"Are You Pregnant?"
Brand Demanded.

His words came out harshly, badly, as an accusation.

She flinched and paled, leaning back against the window frame. "I don't know yet," she whispered. Glancing away, she bit her lip.

Her words hit him like a blow. Whatever he'd expected to hear, he wasn't prepared for that. "Did you plan it?" he asked softly.

He sucked a slow breath, hoping—praying—she'd deny it. Seconds ticked past, each one like another nail in the coffin holding his dreams.

Deny it, he pleaded silently.

She stared at the floor, then lifted her head. "Yes."

Air gushed from his chest, like blood from a wound.

"Why me?" It hurt to say the words.

She squared her shoulders. "Look, I'm sorry for involving you. It wasn't...personal."

Ignoring what looked like fear in her eyes, he lost control. "Not personal! Lady, I was inside you, and I'm the only man w~~ ~~ pretty damned *perso~~

Dear Reader,

Welcome to Silhouette Desire! This month we've created a brand-new lineup of passionate, powerful and provocative love stories just for you.

Begin your reading enjoyment with *Ride the Thunder* by Lindsay McKenna, the September MAN OF THE MONTH and the second book in this beloved author's cross-line series, MORGAN'S MERCENARIES: ULTIMATE RESCUE. An amnesiac husband recovers his memory and returns to his wife and child in *The Secret Baby Bond* by Cindy Gerard, the ninth title in our compelling DYNASTIES: THE CONNELLYS continuity series.

Watch a feisty beauty fall for a wealthy lawman in *The Sheriff & the Amnesiac* by Ryanne Corey. Then meet the next generation of MacAllisters in *Plain Jane MacAllister* by Joan Elliott Pickart, the newest title in THE BABY BET: MacALLISTER'S GIFTS.

A night of passion leads to a marriage of convenience between a gutsy heiress and a macho rodeo cowboy in *Expecting Brand's Baby*, by debut Desire author Emilie Rose. And in Katherine Garbera's new title, *The Tycoon's Lady* falls off the stage into his arms at a bachelorette auction, as part of our popular BRIDAL BID theme promotion.

Savor all six of these sensational new romances from Silhouette Desire today.

Enjoy!

Joan Marlow Golan

Joan Marlow Golan
Senior Editor, Silhouette Desire

Please address questions and book requests to:
Silhouette Reader Service
U.S.: 3010 Walden Ave., P.O. Box 1325, Buffalo, NY 14269
Canadian: P.O. Box 609, Fort Erie, Ont. L2A 5X3

Expecting
Brand's Baby
EMILIE ROSE

Published by Silhouette Books

America's Publisher of Contemporary Romance

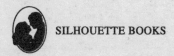

SILHOUETTE BOOKS

ISBN 0-373-76463-4

EXPECTING BRAND'S BABY

Copyright © 2002 by Emilie Rose Cunningham

This edition published by arrangement with Harlequin Books S.A.

® and TM are trademarks of Harlequin Books S.A., used under license.
Trademarks indicated with ® are registered in the United States Patent
and Trademark Office, the Canadian Trade Marks Office and in other
countries.

Visit Silhouette at www.eHarlequin.com

Printed in U.S.A.

EMILIE ROSE

resides in North Carolina with her college sweetheart hus-band and four sons. Her love of romance novels started when she was twelve years old and her mother hid them under the sofa cushions each time Emilie entered the room. Emilie grew up riding and showing horses, and her hobbies include quilting, cooking (especially cheesecake) and anything cowboy. Emilie is an avid Little League mom, and during the season can usually be found on the bleachers watching one of her kids play. When she can spare time for TV, she enjoys the Discovery Channel's medical programs, *ER, CSI* and *Boston Public*. She loves country music because she believes there's a book in every song.

Thanks to my mom, for being the greatest cheerleader a girl could ever have, and to my husband for keeping me in the game when I was too discouraged to continue. I want to thank my kids for learning to cook. I guess you had to, since I forget to feed you when I'm writing. ☺

A special thanks to Sarah Winn,
my pioneering friend, who isn't afraid
to give me a kick in the pants when I need it.

One

She'd save the ranch tonight—even if she had to do it flat on her back.

Toni Swenson chewed her lip and studied the stream of people wearing jeans and cowboy hats flowing toward the National Finals Rodeo. Somewhere inside the arena there had to be a man with the kind of genes she needed. Genes, which would contribute the love of horses, cattle and open spaces to her son.

And it had better be a son, she thought, wiping her brow.

Toni herded along with the rest of the crowd. She swallowed to ease her dry mouth and wiped her damp palms on her jeans. Her heartbeat thundered like a stampede, nearly deafening her. Glancing wistfully back toward the exit, she took a shuddery breath, trying to pull oxygen past the invisible lariat tightening around her neck. Familiar scents and sounds surrounded her: barbecue and nachos, dirt and livestock. A combination unique to the rodeo.

Memories of happier times with her grandfather rushed

at her and pulled her forward when her feet wanted to drag. Why had he died? The ache in her heart increased. And why had he felt the need to put this metaphorical gun to her head and force her to do something totally against her moral beliefs? He, more than anyone, knew why she didn't trust men.

Sliding into her hard-backed aisle seat, Toni wiped her eyes and wondered how she could have stayed away from the sport of rodeo so long. Vet school had been difficult, but surely if she'd tried harder she could have found the time to attend a rodeo or two with her grandfather. Year after year her grandfather had brought her here, put her in her seat and ordered her not to move. A bitter smile twisted her lips. She'd rarely obeyed that directive. Once he'd disappeared toward the chutes, Toni had followed, staying out of his line of vision.

Cowboys and livestock fascinated her. Always had. Tonight, a rootless cowboy who carelessly used and discarded women was exactly what she had to find. It wasn't as if she had a choice.

A whiskey-rough voice drew her gaze to a pair of cowboys coming down the aisle. "Remember the basics. Shoulders square. Free hand in front of you. Run like hell when you hit the ground. You'll do fine."

The dark-haired one with the bedroom voice slapped the younger man on the back. Thick muscles shifted in his forearm. Toni shivered. Arms like that could do serious damage in a fit of rage. He paused in the aisle beside her, waiting while his companion spoke to someone in the stands.

Black leather chaps framed the best backside Toni'd ever laid eyes on. She could scarcely miss the firm glutes and lean thighs parked just inches from the tip of her nose. All those tight muscles were wrapped in denim so snug he might burst a seam riding tonight. And he would ride. The number between his broad shoulders marked him as a competitor. The intensity of his voice labeled him as the winner even before the contest began.

He turned, allowing someone to pass. Toni sat back and shifted her gaze upward. It was either that or look at... something a lady shouldn't stare at. Of course, a lady wouldn't be planning the kind of encounter she had in mind for tonight, either. But if she wanted to hold on to the ranch she'd forget her principles.

The cowboy's gaze brushed over the crowd, landing on her with the force of a hoof in the stomach. She couldn't breathe and wondered if she'd pass out before he looked away. Those dark eyes beneath the brim of his black hat made her heart misbehave and her midsection flutter. His lean face could've jumped straight out of her fantasies. Sharp angles, square jaw, and high cheekbones. This was a devil of a good-looking cowboy. A man in control. Definitely *not* what she'd come for tonight.

She broke eye contact and looked past him toward his young, blue-eyed companion. Now, *that* was the kind of guy she needed. Someone carefree and careless, whose happy-go-lucky manner was as apparent as the dark cowboy's take-charge attitude.

The blonde glanced her way. Toni forced her lips into what she hoped was a come-hither smile and fought the nervous urge to puke into her popcorn box. Blushing furiously, the young man turned away. Toni frowned and peeked at the dark cowboy. He'd witnessed her strikeout and was scowling at her. Heat flooded her cheeks. She'd bet Tall, Dark and Gorgeous had never struck out. Charisma oozed from his pores. No doubt he knew it.

Toni studied the scuffed toes of her boots and pulled in a deep breath. *Remember what's at stake. Remember the mission.* The ranch meant too much to her to back down now. She set her jaw, thrust her shoulders back. She stood, intent on introducing herself to the younger man, but the black-haired devil had already hustled her quarry down the aisle toward the stairs.

With an admiring look at his retreating derriere, she shook her head. No man should look that good. It wasn't fair to the female population—especially the ones like her, who wanted someone easier to handle. Toni gritted her teeth and followed. She couldn't—wouldn't—chicken out tonight. Looks weren't the only things passed along on the DNA. She needed cowboy genes.

A rueful smile twisted Brand's lips. He adjusted the brim of his hat. *Brandon Lander, you're getting too old for this business.* That li'l buckle bunny had barely spared him one glance from her baby blues. She'd been too busy flirting with Bobby Lee. Hell, Bobby was barely nineteen, still a virgin, and planning to stay that way until he married his high-school sweetheart after Christmas. He wouldn't know what to do with a woman like her.

Glancing over his shoulder as he turned toward the chutes, he spotted the blonde tailing 'em. Looked like she had designs on the kid's virtue. Least he could do was help the kid resist temptation. He gave Bobby Lee a shove. "Hustle up. You'll be late. I'll be along directly. I don't ride for a while yet."

Wiping the smile from his face, he turned to confront the woman who seemed determined to lead a young man down the road to hell. With all those curves, it'd be a scenic trip. She was a tiny one, probably weighed little more than a good saddle. She looked fragile, the type some men would want to coddle and protect. But not him.

Fat, buttery curls floated over her shoulders to the tips of her breasts, framing an angelic face. Skin as smooth as the magnolia blossoms growing beside the front porch back home made his fingers itch to touch. No doubt her mouth would've looked like a rosebud if she hadn't mashed it into such a determined line. It irked Brand more than a little that her huge blue eyes looked straight past him and locked on Bobby Lee's back.

The fierce concentration on her features surprised him. She looked like a woman on a quest. He'd seen the same intense expression on many a bull rider just before they left the chute to face a ride that could mean life or death. But what kind of quest would lead a pixie like her behind the chutes? Determined to find out he stepped into her path and tipped his hat.

"Hello, li'l lady. Where you headed?" If her scowl was any gauge, Brand figured she didn't like being called little.

"Excuse me." She tried to step around him, but he widened his stance and looped his thumbs in his belt. She glanced briefly at his World Championship belt buckle. It didn't seem to impress her. She stepped right and Brand sidled left, blocking her. She moved again, and he countered like a good cutting horse.

"I need to pass." Those rosy lips pinched tighter and her face flushed. She gave her curls a toss. "Move, cowboy."

"Can't let you back there, darlin'. Bull riders only." Damn, she was pretty. He took a minute to savor her sweetly curved form, working his way from her tapping toes to the sparks shooting from her eyes. There'd been a time when he'd let himself be distracted by a morsel like her, but not anymore. Her kind spelled trouble. In capital letters.

"Then there are a few riders not listed in my program."

"Aw, darlin', those are just wives and girlfriends. You with one of the fellas?" She wasn't. Bull riders were a close-knit group, and if she'd belonged to any one of his buddies, they'd have been braying like a jackass, wanting everybody to know.

She swallowed hard and stiffened her shoulders. Some of the pink faded from her cheeks. "Not yet."

The news shouldn't have pleased him, but it did. *Which only goes to show you where your brain is tonight, Romeo.* "Look, darlin', we're fixin' to ride. Why don't you head on back up to your seat before you distract somebody and get 'em hurt."

Her face flushed and her chin lifted. "Why don't *you* move before you get hurt?"

Brand coughed to cover his chuckle. So she wanted to play tough? "Do you honestly think I'd be intimidated by a hundred pounds of fluff when my job is to ride a ton of crazy beef?" He faked a shudder. "You got me shakin' in my boots, darlin'."

She eyed his crotch—not in a complimentary way—and shifted her weight. She looked angry enough to end his reproductive years before he put 'em to good use. Brand rolled to the balls of his feet, prepared to dodge her knee.

"Wish me luck, Brand." Bobby Lee's yell distracted her and gave Brand a chance to shuffle back a step or two.

Keeping a wary eye on the angel with an attitude, he gave Bobby Lee a thumbs-up. The kid, one of the lowest scorers to make the finals, waved and turned toward the chute. It was a matter of pride that as the high scorer, Brand would be riding last. Still, he had a lot riding on his last go and couldn't afford to be distracted by a spunky angel. He considered asking one of the ushers to show her back to her seat, but hesitated, somehow reluctant to turn the spitfire loose.

Toni scowled at the broad-shouldered man blocking her path. Thanks to him, she'd missed her chance to meet the potential father of her baby. Another clean-cut cowboy sidled up, but the band on his ring finger disqualified him. She sighed. Lady Luck was not with her and time was running out.

"Hey Brand, a bunch of us are gettin' together to down a few later. Bobby Lee's coming. How 'bout you?"

Toni straightened when he named the bar of the hotel where she was staying. Maybe all was not lost.

Dark eyes narrowed on her for a moment. "I'll be there."

Toni fought the urge to squirm beneath the challenging stare. The announcer called Bobby Lee something-or-another's name. Toni shifted her gaze to her quarry in an attempt to break free of the devil's spell. If the young cowboy in the chute was going to father her child, she ought to know his last name—if for no other reason than to avoid him after tonight.

The metal gate opened with a clang. Hooves, arena dirt and bull exploded into the air and the crowd went wild. Toni caught herself looking at the pushy dark-haired cowboy instead of at Bobby Lee. He moved closer to the ring, staring intently at the bull and rider. His right hand clenched in front of him, as if he were holding the rigging and living the ride himself. Something about his total concentration on bull and rider, something about *him* held her attention. Powerful muscles bunched and shifted in his forearm and beneath his shirt and jeans.

The noise of the crowd drowned out her pounding heart. *Leave while the devil is distracted.* Her feet didn't move. She blamed her strange fascination on the fact that the cowboy's thick drawl and lazy attitude hadn't seemed to fit the intelligence and the intensity she'd seen in his eyes. She didn't want to notice that anymore than she wanted to admit he was easily the sexiest man she'd ever laid eyes on.

Remember the mission. He isn't what you need tonight, or any other night for that matter. He's too big, too strong, too physical. A man like him could seriously hurt a woman. The hairs on her arms rose. She needed the easygoing cowboy clinging to the back of the bull bounding around the arena. And she only needed *him* for about thirty minutes.

Toni took a step back. Maybe Providence had smiled on her plan after all. It was the right time of the month for her to conceive this child her grandfather's will insisted she bear, and the man who could help her do it would be coming straight to her hotel. She could meet him in the hotel bar—only twelve floors away from conception.

She *would* succeed tonight. Tomorrow she'd leave

Las Vegas carrying the seed of her future and her link to the past.

It was the only way to hold on to her sanctuary.

Watching the door, Toni tore her cocktail napkin into thin strips. She sipped her drink and considered slinking off to her room alone. All too soon the boisterous cowboys came through the swinging doors with Mr. Wrong leading the way. Her stomach lurched. Toni leaned forward in her seat to see if Bobby Lee was in the pack and there he was. Suddenly, she felt nauseous. Women followed the men, enlarging their number to nearly a dozen.

The dark cowboy—Brand, they'd called him—seemed to be the center of attention. People patted him on the back as he passed. Hooking an arm around Bobby Lee's head, he gave him a playful noogie.

He glanced up, his dark gaze locking onto hers with the intensity of a bull preparing to charge. She struggled to pull air past the knot in her throat and tugged at the low-cut neckline of the tacky black dress she'd bought in the hotel boutique. Brand's eyes shifted downward. She wanted to cover her overexposed cleavage, but fastened her hands around her glass instead. The dress was a necessary costume for the role she had to play tonight. Seductress was a new one for her.

Brand said something, and the group shifted like a herd of cattle and headed in her direction. The moment of truth had arrived. Toni's heart thumped. She had to do this. *Had to.* She chased the lump in her throat with another sip of margarita and forced herself to look beyond Brand to Bobby Lee.

She smiled, even though it felt as if it would crack the makeup she'd shoveled on, then patted her upswept hair. One sneeze would have the whole mess tumbling down. Toni fought to subdue the hysterical giggle squirming in her chest and aimed for a take-me-to-bed expression.

Brand bent his head toward Bobby Lee. Whatever he

said caused the younger man to blush and drop back a step. Long before she was ready, the group hovered beside the semicircular booth. Brand winked and flashed her a heart-stopping grin.

"Hello, darlin'. Thanks for savin' us a table." Without waiting for an invitation, he gestured for his friends to sit down and slid into the booth beside her. He stretched his arm along the back of the banquette.

Another cowboy scooted in on Toni's left, crunching her against Brand's hard thighs and into the crook of his arm. Heat seared her. She jerked forward.

With a calloused finger, Brand traced a light pattern on her bare nape. A shiver skipped down her spine. Toni stiffened and tried to shift away, but another bump from the man on her left hemmed her in. Trapped.

She glared at Brand and hissed, "Give me some room."

His teeth gleamed, straight and white. As potent as a caress, his gaze drifted from her eyes, to her lips, to her cleavage. Toni's nipples peaked in betrayal. She wouldn't make a scene by screaming at the pushy cowboy. That wouldn't gain her any points with Bobby Lee who obviously worshipped the jerk. She inhaled slowly, hoping to calm her racing pulse.

Brand smelled of cinnamon and cedar rather than the sweaty bull and arena dirt she'd come to expect from rodeo cowboys. He'd traded the bold striped shirt he'd worn earlier for another, this one resembling an American flag.

She wouldn't let a nice-smelling cowboy with a penchant for loud shirts distract her from her mission. She surveyed the others, dismayed to see Bobby Lee far down the table. With several people between them, she couldn't speak to him without yelling. Brand and the beefy man had her boxed in, so moving closer was out. How in the heck would she woo Bobby Lee with her new Wonderbra from this distance?

Damn. Her first attempt at seduction shot down.

The waitress appeared and nodded toward Toni's empty glass. "What'll ya have, hon? Another one of those?"

No matter how much Dutch courage she needed, she wouldn't accomplish tonight's chore if she passed out first. She shook her head. "Iced tea this time, please."

After giving his order, the beefy cowboy to her left leaned over her, practically pushing Toni into Brand's lap. Obviously, *he* enjoyed the effects of her new lingerie. "What? No champagne, Brand? You ain't celebrating?"

"How many is that now? Three?" A woman with artificial everything reached across the table to scrape an acrylic nail across the back of Brand's hand.

Toni gripped her glass. It wasn't like her to be bitchy, but she'd bet good money that neither the woman's hair nor breasts were compliments of Mother Nature.

"Four." Brand drew his hand out of the talon's reach and threaded his fingers through Toni's. She startled and tried to extricate herself from his warm, calloused grip, to no avail. Sparks hopped and skipped up her arm. His hands were huge with a multitude of tiny scars across the backs and knuckles. Like a fighter's. She hated the telling tremor invading her limbs.

The mission.

The waitress returned. She winked at Brand and set a tall glass in front of him on a cocktail napkin that had a phone number scribbled in the corner. "The bartender sent over something special for you, Champ. Here's your tea, hon."

Toni waited for Brand to acknowledge the blatant invitation in the waitress's smile. When he didn't, the waitress distributed the rest of the order.

"You gonna quit now?" Silence fell over the table after Bobby Lee's question.

Brand drummed the fingers of his free hand on the table. "Might. If I can find a place I can run by myself."

"Tired of taking orders, huh? How many brothers you got back home bossin' you around?" Bobby Lee asked.

"Too many, and damn straight, I'm tired of taking orders. Between them and my dad the ranch is at least a decade behind the times." Brand raised his glass.

Bobby Lee grinned. "How about if I send some of my sisters down to meet your brothers? I know Mom and Dad would be happy to have at least a couple of 'em out of the house."

Toni grimaced into her glass. She knew genetics, and this wasn't good news. If Bobby Lee came from a predominantly female family, her chances of having a son with him were slimmer than say…if she bedded a fella with brothers. A major hitch in her plan.

She couldn't think of an alternative—couldn't think period, because from shoulder to knee, Brand lived up to his name. Surely, there would be singe marks along her side. She tried to move so that at least some part of her wasn't plastered against lean, hard cowboy.

Another cowboy hailed them from across the room. He joined the group, squeezing into the booth. The gap she'd fought to put between her and Brand vanished. To make matters worse, Brand hooked his arm around her shoulder and pulled her even closer. She held her breath and arched as far away as possible.

Distracted by the strength of the hand cupping her shoulder and the cinnamony breath stirring the curls on her neck, Toni missed nearly all of the names bandied about. Hyperventilation threatened. She tried to shrug him off.

The thickheaded devil gave her a squeeze and shifted his fingers to massage her neck with a deft touch. "Loosen up. You've got knots the size of my fist back here."

Her traitorous spine nearly melted. Toni lifted her glass and downed half of the cloudy liquid. It burned going down like no iced tea she'd ever had. Maybe the water was different in Vegas? She sniffed the glass. Was that bourbon in her drink or was it the beefy guy's breath? He was drooling over her cleavage again. She put an elbow in his ribs.

Nursing her drink, she searched for a way out of her predicament. Should she risk fouling up the plan with Bobby Lee or look for another sperm donor with a predominantly male family?

One like Brand.

No, no, no, he was definitely not what she was looking for. No doubt he'd make the ordeal ahead memorable— heaven knows his fingers on her nape were addling her brain—but something in those sharp eyes of his told her he didn't have a careless bone in his body, despite his profession. He wouldn't forget something as important as protection. She set her glass down. It rattled against the table. What a mess. Her ranch was on the line and her hormones were in an uproar for *the wrong man.*

She'd loved dear old Gramps, and she missed him terribly, but he'd landed her in a mess. Under the terms of Gramps's will she could lose her legacy, her sanctuary, land that had been in her family for generations, because she was female. Her grandfather had insisted a male inherit. A husband or a child. Toni had neither. She loved kids, but a husband...no way.

What if she ended up with a husband like her father, who had proved his point with his fists, or one who'd take the ranch from her if the marriage failed? Her lawyer had joked during their hasty phone call that settling the estate would be a lot easier if Toni were pregnant. The idea had taken off like a wild pony and led her here. She'd do anything to hold on to the one place where she'd always felt safe—even sleep with a stranger.

The beefy guy winked and leered. "I'm a calf roper, sweetheart. I'm fast with a rope and good with my hands. I like to tie 'em up."

From the gleam in his eyes she didn't think he meant just calves. She scowled at him over her glass. Brand glared and the man shrank back.

"You left." Brand's whiskey-rough voice murmured in her ear.

Toni choked on her drink and jerked her head around to find dark eyes just inches from her own. She wheezed. Brand patted then stroked her back. The fire licking up her vertebrae had nothing whatsoever to do with the liquid she'd consumed.

"You mean you didn't see Brand ride?" somebody at the table asked before she could catch her breath. Or her wits.

The hovering waitress offered Toni a sympathetic smile. "Probably couldn't stand it, could you, sugar?"

Somehow these people were under the impression that she and Brand were a couple. Since he was wrapped around her like kudzu, it wasn't a far-out conclusion. To get any closer, he'd have to be a tattoo. If she wanted to end the night in bed with Bobby Lee, she had to straighten them out. "Look—"

"What'd you say your name was?" the silicone woman asked.

"Ah…Toni. But—"

"Brand's sure kept you a secret," she interrupted.

"That's because—"

Brand put a finger to her lips. "We wanted to lock ourselves in the hotel room once the rodeo was over. Not coming out for a week." His waggling brows drew snickers from his friends.

Stunned, Toni swiveled. The damned devil had just ruined everything. He snatched his finger away before she could bite him. "What did you say?"

He grinned. "Sorry, I let the cat out of the bag. I'd get down on my knees and beg you to take me on up to bed, darlin', but it'd be kind of painful. Caught one of 'em on the gate."

His eyes weren't black, she discovered. They were the color of dark Godiva chocolate with lighter flecks of milk chocolate drizzled over the top. Good thing Godiva was out of her price range. Chocolate was the one thing she couldn't resist.

"You...I..." The tug of an unwanted attraction erased whatever she'd been trying to say. She closed her eyes. *Too big. Too strong. The mission.*

"You're right. I should've kept our secret." He shrugged his impossibly wide shoulders and stroked a calloused finger over her cheek. Toni turned into a vessel of rampant hormones. What was it about him that did this to her? "I'm just a dumb cowboy, darlin'."

His humility was patently insincere. She stifled the urge to dump the rest of her drink in his lap and pressed the cold glass to the fire he'd left on her cheek. If he'd wanted to spoil her chances with the other cowboys, he couldn't have chosen a better way than marking her as his. Even if she could ditch this irritating bull jockey, she no longer stood a chance with Bobby Lee or any other man at the table—except maybe the beefy calf roper. She grimaced and downed the remainder of her drink. She might be desperate, but she wasn't that desperate. She wanted a few words with this Brand character for screwing up her carefully thought-out plan. *"Out!"*

"You're wanting to test the mattress already?" Innocence personified, Brand batted his ridiculously lush eyelashes.

She'd kill him. "Let me out!"

"All right, darlin', but it's no rush. We've got all night." Capturing an errant curl, he twined it around his finger and added in a sexy whisper, "I promise I'll be worth the wait."

Fury vibrated through her. Awareness made it difficult to think. Damn the devil's sorry hide. She shoved him hard enough to move a horse. Brand didn't budge, but her fingers ended up buried in his chest. His firm, warm muscles contracted beneath her fingertips and Toni felt an insane urge to dig in. "I said, let me out."

"Well, folks, the li'l lady wants me naked. Thanks for

the party, but drinks are on me tonight.'' Brand stood, pulled out his wallet, and tossed a couple of hundred-dollar bills on the table. He tipped his hat, then grabbed Toni's hand and tugged her out of the bar to a chorus of raucous comments.

Cursing him under her breath, she stumbled after him. Her knees seemed to be working without direction from her head and when he stopped she fell into him. She wasn't drunk, but she was as close to it as she'd ever been in her entire life.

"Are you crazy?" She planted her feet in the lobby.

"It's not me that's crazy, darlin'. You're eyeing Bobby Lee like a starving dog eyes a bone. He's not on the menu."

Was this macho jerk in the tacky shirt calling her a dog? She ought to kick him in the—

"He's engaged and staying that way." Another group of cowboys burst through the front door of the hotel. One called his name. Brand swore and scooped her into his arms.

Her head spun. Afraid he'd drop her, Toni clung to his broad shoulders. He didn't stop moving until they were behind a bank of plants beside the elevators. The doors pinged open. Brand ducked inside and dropped her legs. She slid against him until her feet touched the floor. Toni couldn't turn him loose. The elevator whisked upward, leaving her stomach behind. Grasping his thick leather belt, she struggled for balance. She lifted her head to give him a piece of her mind, but choked back the words when the doors opened again. Several couples crowded inside.

One of the men gestured to the unlit numbers on the panel. "Which floor?"

Toni gave her floor number automatically and immediately regretted it when Brand gave her a smug smile. Fine. She'd take him to her room, tear a strip off his obnoxiously overconfident hide, then she'd go back downstairs and do what she had to do. If she couldn't have Bobby Lee, there were a dozen other cowboys to choose from. With any luck she'd find one with an abundance of brothers.

She'd bet the ranch—and essentially that was what she was doing—that she could find a cowboy who'd let her have things her way. One who would be careless. And she'd start looking for him just as soon as she ditched this hardheaded bull rider.

The doors opened and Toni stepped out. Brand caught her elbow and followed closer than her shadow until she stopped in front of her door. With an irritated glare over her shoulder, Toni tried to stuff the key card through the slot but her hands were shaking too much. Brand took the card from her and reached around her to insert it into the lock. He crowded her, enclosing her in his scent, his heat. When he opened the door, Toni raced through, praying Brand wouldn't follow.

No such luck.

Two

Brand followed the hell-bent angel into her room, unable to stop himself from admiring the delicious curve of her backside in the tight dress and the first-class set of legs below the short hem. He blew a silent whistle. Toni might be petite, but everything was in the right place.

She wanted sex. No doubt about it. A woman didn't dress in fabric tight enough to reveal the dimple of her navel if she didn't want a guy to go peeling it off her. *Real slow*. His fingers flexed in anticipation, but he reined in his maverick thoughts. He wasn't here for a horizontal two-step.

Evidently, she had a thing for bull riders. He'd seen and resisted women like her dozens of times over the past ten years. Buckle bunnies weren't his thing, but for once, he wished they were, because this one.... Whew. Pure temptation.

He nudged back his hat and scratched his brow. So why in the hell had he followed her up here? Was his pride tweaked because she'd ignored him? Probably. Women usually swarmed him like flies on a fresh cowpie. Was it the need to let off some steam after winning his fourth world championship? Nah, if that was the case he wouldn't have left his friends in the bar.

Was he really trying to save Bobby Lee from her clutches? He had a soft spot for the kid who reminded him a lot of his youngest brother. Bobby Lee had the same idealistic view of life, the same certainty that everybody was a kindhearted soul. He'd be easy prey for a woman on the make, regardless of his fiancée, and Toni had all the markings of a woman on the make.

Brand rubbed the prickle at the back of his neck. He had a feeling he was here for purely selfish reasons. Like the need to taste her lips. Were they as soft as they'd looked before she smeared that red lipstick on 'em? Or was it the need to test the silkiness of the magnolia skin she'd hidden beneath a truckload of makeup? His hands tingled with the need to take the pins from her buttery curls and feel them drag across his bare chest. He wondered if the heady scent of dew-covered roses was stronger between her breasts, between her legs.

He wanted her, dammit, in a way he'd never wanted before.

She stalked halfway across the room and back. A pint-size bundle of dynamite. He'd swear that beneath all the stuff on her face, her cheeks were flushed. Her breasts rose and fell swiftly, nearly bursting from the low neckline of her dress. Brand hoped she'd breathe a little harder.

She flung her tiny purse onto the sofa and parked her clenched fists on her hips. "You are a total jerk."

Not exactly the invitation to her bed he'd expected, but he could handle 'em feisty. He fought a grin. "Who me?"

"You. You've ruined everything with your buttinsky ways."

She sounded near tears. Brand's heart twisted. He couldn't stand a woman crying. "Look, darlin'—"

"I am not your darlin'. You are not what I'm looking for, and I want you to get lost." She paced to the window and back.

Tears streaked mascara down her cheeks.

"Look, dar—" She sucked a sharp breath and almost popped out of the dress, distracting him so much he nearly missed her glare. He pulled off his hat and tossed it onto the dresser, then shoved his hands through his hair. "Ah, Toni? Bobby Lee's a good kid. He wouldn't know how to handle a woman like you."

"And I suppose you would?" She wiped a hand across her face, smearing her mascara in an inch-wide trail. When she caught sight of the black on the back of her hand, she gave a startled cry and looked in the mirror. Cussing like a cowboy, she hustled toward the bathroom.

The lady had an interesting vocabulary. Brand shook his head. Over his chuckles, he heard water running. When Toni came back into the room, her smooth skin was free of makeup. She still wore the hooker's dress, and her hair still looked like she'd spent a long, hot night in some lucky man's bed.

"Go. Away." She sank onto the edge of the bed and buried her face in her hands. "I have something to do tonight, and you're messing it up."

Brand studied the defeated droop of her shoulders. "If I leave, are you going back downstairs?"

Her shoulders squared and she lifted her chin. When she met his gaze it was pure grit and determination he saw in her baby blues. He wondered what put it there. "I have to."

He ought to leave, but he couldn't seem to get his feet to head out the door. Against his better judgment, Brand sat beside her on the bed and twined a curl around his finger. He tugged until her lips were within an inch of his. "And if I don't go?"

Her eyes rounded. He heard her breath catch and his did the same. It locked in his chest with a painful burn. She exhaled, her breath sweeping across his lips like a butterfly wing. Brand's head spun. His heart and groin throbbed in tandem. He wanted to blame it on the drink he'd had downstairs, but Toni'd had him on his ear back at the arena when she hadn't been wearing a bucket of makeup, and he'd been stone-cold sober.

"You should leave." Her voice was a whisper, but her eyes focused on his mouth. His lips tingled, anticipating the kiss he couldn't do without. Brand traced a path from her silky shoulder to her slender wrist with a surprisingly unsteady hand. He captured her fingers and spread them over his pounding heart.

"Yep, but I sure don't want to." He tugged the curl, closing the distance between her lips and his. Soft as a rosebud. Sweet as a sugar cube. She hit him like the dose of pure oxygen the medics gave after a nasty toss. He brushed her lips once, twice. Already he was addicted to the taste of her. He had to be out of his mind because there was no way he was leaving.

"Darlin', there's nothing you can find downstairs that I can't give you."

She drew back and studied him for several unblinking moments. Unshed tears glistened in her eyes. And secrets. Brand drew back a fraction.

"You married?" He wouldn't sleep with another man's woman.

Her eyes widened. "No."

"Me, neither. And I don't aim to get that way. Ever." She swallowed, then nodded. "Me, neither."

Brand pulled a pin from her hair. When she offered no resistance, he threaded his fingers through the silky strands, removing the rest of the pins and dropping them on the floor. The fat curls wrapped around his wrist and tumbled over her shoulders as he ran his fingers through the tangles. Her head lolled back, baring her throat.

Brand bent and pressed his lips to the rapidly beating pulse at the base of her neck. If he had good sense he'd get the hell out of here. His good sense wasn't listening. "You know what I want, don't you, Toni?"

He drew back to look at her flushed face. Her lids lifted slowly. Desire slumbered in her eyes. She nodded and moistened her lips.

"I want to make love to you. I want to taste every inch of you, starting right here." Brand nipped her earlobe. She pulled in a shuddery breath then exhaled on a sigh. He stroked his palm across her smooth cheek. She nuzzled into it. "You want that, too?"

"Yes."

Brand felt a moment's hesitation at the surprise in her voice. If she hadn't wanted him, then why had she brought him to her room? She pressed her lips to his palm and suddenly, it didn't matter. Tugging his wallet from his jeans, he withdrew a string of foil packets and tossed them on the bed. He'd picked 'em up for one of the other guys, but…tough.

Toni's mouth opened then closed, as if she'd had something to say then changed her mind. She fisted a hand in his shirt. Brand forgot all reason and lowered his head.

He overwhelmed her with his soft, experimental kisses. Toni thought she'd turn into a blazing inferno if he did that thing with his tongue again. He did and she nearly combusted on the spot. Alarmed by her body's enthusiastic response, Toni pushed him away and stared at him. What she was doing was wrong. She shouldn't enjoy it this much, but the way he made her feel was…incredible. He was so gentle and yet his hunger for her was unmistakable.

"Easy, darlin'. Take it easy." Brand nuzzled her neck, and nibbled on her collarbone.

Breathless, Toni grasped for sanity, for control. Her fingers tangled in his hair. When his tongue traced the neckline of her dress her reasons for resisting toppled like a row of dominos. She forgot about holding back. Instead she arched her back and held him close. "Oh…Brand."

He caught the fabric in his teeth and tugged it down to

reveal her strapless black satin bra. Afraid he'd be disappointed because the bra promised more of her than there actually was, Toni tried to cover herself. He caught her wrists.

"I need to taste you, Toni. In the worst kind of way."

She hesitated, but the desire blazing in his eyes convinced her to lower her hands. She felt peculiar, as if every nerve ending she possessed hungered for his touch. He scorched her mouth with another incendiary kiss.

"Zipper?"

She shook her head.

"I just peel it off?"

"Mmmmm."

Suiting word to deed, he scrunched the dress around her waist. With a flick of his fingers, the bra dropped. He cupped her breasts, thumbing her nipples. Sparklers blazed from his calloused hands straight to her womb. Toni closed her eyes and let her head fall back. The man had magical hands.

"You can touch me, too." He pulled his shirttails from his pants and yanked the snapped placket apart. Within seconds, the shirt lay on the floor.

Brand had a marvelous chest. A smattering of dark hair dusted his clearly defined pectorals and bisected his taut belly. Toni reached for him, then drew back, afraid her touch would unleash the animal in him. She'd been this far before and been scared out of her wits by her partner's loss of control. She'd ended up locked in the bathroom until he'd gone home.

Brand caught her hand and pressed it to his breast. A flat male nipple prodded her palm like a branding iron. He closed his eyes and inhaled deeply. "Oh, yeah."

His touch remained gentle. He didn't go wild and crush her into the mattress. Tentatively, she tunneled her nails through the dark curls, testing the texture, and loving the way the hairs tickled her palms.

He hissed and pulled her hand away. "Maybe we better wait till next time for that."

Brand didn't give her time to ask why. He bent her over his arm and captured a nipple in his mouth, suckling until she squirmed on the bed. He transferred his attention to her other breast. Like a content cat she clawed the sheets, his hair, his back—not to get free, but in ecstasy. When his lips left her breasts to travel down her abdomen in the wake of her dress she nearly cried. Then the dress was gone and she lay before him in nothing but thigh-high stockings, tiny panties and spike heels.

His gaze poured over her like melted chocolate, evaporating her momentary flash of nerves. Brand made her feel desirable. Sexy. Needy. He stood and leaned against the wall. He shucked one boot, then the other. His socks followed. When his hands fell to his championship belt buckle, Toni closed her eyes. Watching the man undress was more excitement than she could bear. Fabric rustled. Something heavy hit the floor.

Her mouth watered. Her skin tingled. Anticipation of what he'd do to her next left her panting. *You shouldn't be enjoying this.* The thought scattered with the touch of his lips on her ankle. She opened her eyes to find him kneeling beside the bed. Naked. This is where she should panic, but Brand did nothing to alarm her. He removed her shoes, rolled down her stockings, then gently eased her thighs apart. He tasted his way past her calf, her knee, her thigh, to the part of her screaming for his attention. She knew what he planned to do, had read about it in one of her college roommate's erotic novels. She'd even touched herself, but nothing, *nothing* could prepare her for the lightning strike of his tongue. She cried out and slapped a hand over her mouth.

He nipped her thigh. "Don't. I want to hear you scream."

"I—I don't scream." Not in pain or in pleasure.

"You will and you'll love it." He sucked the point of

her desire into his mouth and set her off. Roman candles careened through her bloodstream, and she promptly proved his words.

"That's it, darlin'. Now let's see if you can do it again."

She did, several times. Brand knelt on the bed and reached for a condom. By then, Toni didn't care that he was preventing the very thing she sought. Nor did she fear the size of his enormous erection. Hungrily, she reached for him. He braced himself above her to plunder her mouth, but it wasn't enough. Toni wrapped her legs around his waist and urged him on. Thus far, he'd been gentle, but she no longer needed gentle. He'd done something to her, freed something inside her that she didn't understand.

"Easy, darlin'." He nibbled her ear and the cords of her neck. "We have all night."

"Now."

He chuckled. "Yes, ma'am."

With one deep thrust, he filled her. Toni arched off the bed at the unexpected stab of pain. She'd ridden horses before she walked. She hadn't thought there'd be any sign of her innocence left.

Brand bowed back in surprise. Rolling over without disconnecting their bodies, he cradled her against his chest and stroked her back, her hair. "Relax. Let me know when you're ready."

His sensitivity to her discomfort amazed her. The pain receded and the hunger resumed. Beneath her ear, Brand's chest rose and fell rapidly, his heart raced, but he didn't force her. Tentatively, Toni shifted.

Brand sucked in a sharp breath. His jaw clenched, his hands tightened on her waist. "Good to go?"

"Yeah."

"I wish I could promise you slow, darlin', but—" he shook his head "—you've got me triggered."

He lifted her and eased her back down, filling her again and again. Toni picked up the rhythm until she couldn't move fast enough to satisfy the need in her. When her legs gave out Brand flipped her over and rose above her as they raced toward completion. Toni imploded and Brand followed.

She lay there for a moment trying to figure out how she could have given up control and loved every minute of it. The man had her pinned to the bed. Why wasn't she clawing her way out from under him? Her eyelids grew heavy and she stretched like a satisfied cat. She'd figure out why in a minute…or ten.

Brand rolled to her side. He nuzzled her forehead and kissed her brow. One calloused palm skated down her spine to cup her bottom. He whispered into her ear, "Woman, you ought to be wearing a warning sign."

Toni fell asleep with a smile on her lips.

Her head pounded. Cotton wool filled her mouth. For several seconds, Toni considered burrowing into the warmth behind her and going back to sleep. *Warmth? In December?*

Cautiously, she opened her eyes. A muscle-corded arm pinned her to the mattress. Her heart jolted in panic. Oh, God, she'd done it. Nausea swirled in her stomach. She clapped a hand over her mouth, then checked to make sure she hadn't woken her oblivious partner in crime. Brand. *Brand who?* She didn't even know the man's last name. Shame swept through her.

She eased from beneath the tanned hand cupping her breast. Keeping a wary eye on the occupant of the bed, she gathered jeans and a shirt from the back of the chair. Her bedmate rolled to his back, throwing his arms wide. Toni jumped, but relaxed when his eyes remained closed.

Rumpled hair. Stubble-darkened chin. Thick thighs and muscular calves tangled in the twisted linens. Against her will, her eyes swept over his broad chest and down his flat stomach to the corner of the tumbled sheets covering the crucial parts. She didn't need visuals to remember the silken hard flesh which had brought her so much pleasure

throughout the night or to recall how gentle those big calloused hands had been each time he'd reached for her.

Squeezing her eyes shut, Toni swallowed hard. *Mission
accomplished.* The knowledge gave her no satisfaction.
She'd done the unthinkable to hold on to the ranch. *And
she'd enjoyed every single sinful moment of it.* What kind
of woman did that make her?

She crept into the bathroom and pulled on her clothes,
then studied the woman in the mirror. Other than the red-
dish mark on her neck and the panic in her eyes, she
looked the same, nothing like a woman who'd seduce a
man into forgetting to use a condom. She stuffed her tooth-
brush and paste into her bag because she didn't want to
risk waking the cowboy by running the water. She had to
leave before Brand awoke. She could barely face herself.
She knew she couldn't face him. What she'd done last
night contradicted her moral beliefs. She'd shared her body
with a stranger and stolen something more personal than
money from him. Something much more important.

Easing open the bathroom door, Toni peeked into the
room. On the floor beside the bed, her clothes and his
embraced each other, as tangled together as their bodies
had been last night. Her womb tightened with the memory
of the way Brand had tutored her. Her one-night cowboy
had made a tawdry night beautiful. For that, she'd never
forget him.

How could she have enjoyed it? She cursed her wanton
soul. How could she have forgotten—even for one second—why she was doing what she'd done? She felt a moment's regret for what might have been had they met under
other circumstances. But no, she didn't want to give a man
control of her life again. She'd learned the hard way that
nothing was more important than independence.

Still, there was a heaviness in her heart over how she'd
used the man in the rumpled bed. He didn't deserve it. It
didn't matter that the ranch was the only place she'd felt

safe in her life. She'd used Brand, and now she intended
to toss him aside.

Toni hefted her suitcase. Tears burned her throat. It was
too late for regrets. She opened the door and stopped cold.
Brand's face stared up at her from the front page of the
complimentary newspaper lying on the floor outside her
door. She held her breath and picked up the paper. The
pages rattled in her hand.

Brand Leaves His Mark in Vegas, the caption above the
photo said. Toni's hand fluttered to her heart as she read
the article below.

Brandon Lander clinched his fourth world championship in bull riding last night. The twenty-eight-
year-old cowboy from McMullen County, Texas, has
been on a hot streak during the finals. He not only
rode all ten bulls, but his final ride on Detonator, a
bounty bull unridden all season, netted him a twenty-
five-thousand-dollar bonus.

Friends close to Lander say the champ is considering retirement. Lander could not be reached for
comment, but turning his back on the sport could cost
him a bundle. His endorsements alone total well into
the six-figure range.

"Brand's a friend and mentor to a lot of us younger
guys," says Bobby Lee Garrison, a fellow competitor
and son of Democratic Senator Garrison from
Oklahoma. "What he don't know about a bull ain't
worth knowing. He's got years of good riding ahead
of him."

Toni clutched the paper to her chest. She'd made a huge
mistake. Not only had she ended up with a take-charge
kind of cowboy, she'd picked a famous one who lived less
than two hundred miles from her grandfather's ranch. Of

course, Bobby Lee, a senator's son, would have been worse.

She ran for the elevator as fast as she could. She'd known Brand was trouble from the moment she'd laid eyes on him. He'd drawn her attention from the job at hand. She should have steered clear. She should have known better.

She should have stuck with her plan. Damn. Double damn. She punched the call button again and paced beside the elevators. She'd wanted a rootless man who wouldn't care that he'd forgotten to use protection that last time. She had a feeling Brand wasn't likely to forget.

She'd had every intention of kicking him out last night and going back downstairs to find someone else, but with one kiss, Brand had changed her mind. She was twenty-six years old and had been kissed quite a few times, but she'd only gotten close to becoming intimate with one man. He'd scared her to death by turning into a rabid octopus after a couple of hot kisses and hurt her in his enthusiasm. When she'd asked him to stop he'd turned nasty. She'd decided intimacy wasn't worth the risk.

She hadn't been afraid last night.

Toni squashed the thought. The elevator doors opened and she leaped inside. When Brand didn't appear before the doors closed, she sagged against the wall. Her grandfather's ranch had never seemed more like a refuge. She couldn't wait to get to the only real home she'd ever known.

Brand awoke with a smile on his face. He snuggled deeper into the pillow, inhaling Toni's scent. Damned if the sweet little angel hadn't worn him out. He hadn't been able to get enough of her, nor she of him it seemed. Her hungry kisses and sexy little mews had kept him hard all night.

His chest expanded with pride that she'd allowed him to be her first lover. He'd done his best to make sure she didn't regret it. Despite his concern that she'd be sore, she'd been hungry for him again and again. They'd made love more times than…Brand rocketed up in the bed.

More times than he'd had condoms. "Hell."

The space beside him was empty. Toni's dress lay crumpled on the floor where he'd tossed it. He threw back the covers and stalked into the bathroom to find her. The bathroom was empty and her junk wasn't on the counter. A knot formed in his gut. Swearing, he returned to the bedroom. Her suitcase was gone. With his heart pounding, Brand grabbed the phone and dialed the front desk.

"Miss Swenson checked out."

Brand clenched his fist and rubbed his forehead. "She forgot to leave me a forwarding address. Could you get that for me?"

"I'm not at liberty to release that information, sir."

"Lady, I'm calling from her room. She'd want me to have her address."

"I'm sorry, sir."

Slamming the phone down, he jabbed his hands through his hair and yanked on his clothes. "Ow, ow, ow." He rubbed his tender knee and threw his boot across the room. It hit the wall with a satisfying thunk. He'd been had. How many times had he warned the younger guys about just such a thing? And he'd been stupid enough to forget protection at least once.

From the beginning, he'd thought the woman was on a quest. He'd seen the determination in her eyes and the set of her delicate chin. But had he paid attention? *Hell, no.* It had been a damn long time since he'd had a woman, and he'd let his hormones lead him straight into trouble.

What did she want? Money? He pulled out his wallet and counted the stack of bills. All there. No, that didn't make sense, anyway. If she'd wanted money, why had she been gunning for Bobby Lee? Why not him? With all his endorsements, he was worth a hell of a lot more than Bobby Lee. He pulled on his boots. Maybe it wasn't money she was after. More than one of Bobby Lee's relatives held an elected office. Did she want to cause a political scandal? Brand scrubbed a hand over his beard-stubbled face and cradled his head. She hadn't gone to bed with Bobby Lee.

What in the hell did it mean? What did she want?

Shoving his hat on his pounding head, Brand let himself into the hall. Too antsy to wait for the elevator, he headed for the stairs, banged-up knee and all. Ignoring the pain, he raced to his own room three floors up and burst through the door.

"Wha— What is it?" Bobby Lee sat up in bed and eyed him groggily. Man, the kid didn't even need to shave every morning. What could she have wanted with such an innocent?

"Have you heard from Toni this morning?"

Bobby Lee blushed and studied the sheets. "Nah, I thought she was…that you had…you were, like together."

"We were. I need a private detective." Brand started flinging off his clothes as he headed for the bathroom.

"What for?" The kid rubbed his eyes like a two-year-old.

Naked, Brand paused in the bathroom doorway. "Toni lit out of here. I need to find her."

"She steal your wallet or something?"

Brand's stomach clenched and bile burned the back of his throat. She'd taken more than his possessions. The woman was carrying his seed. It was a damned old-fashioned way of thinking, but he was going to track her down and make sure that he hadn't made her pregnant. If he had… He rubbed his face. If he had, then the Lander family history was going to repeat itself. "Or something."

Bobby stretched his bowlegged, bony frame. "My dad has a P.I. he uses every now and then. She'll find your man, uh, woman."

Bobby Lee talked to his father and scribbled across a piece of hotel stationery. He hung up the phone and passed the paper to Brand. "You gonna marry her once you find her?"

To Bobby Lee, sex and marriage went hand in hand. Brand hated to disillusion the kid. Why had he gone to bed with Toni? He hadn't intended to. He'd just wanted to spoil her chances with any other slobbering cowboy. Now there was the possibility of a pregnancy. And marriage. He headed for the shower.

"Damned if I know, kid."

Three

Toni drove from Vegas to her apartment. After a few fretful hours sleep she loaded her belongings into a rented trailer and turned in her keys. If things went according to plan, she was going home to the Rocking A for good. No more packing or hiding.

She refused to consider the possibility that she might have failed in her mission. After what she'd done, she had to be pregnant with Brand Lander's child. A son, she hoped. A daughter wouldn't be loved any less, but it wouldn't solve her problem. Her stomach lurched. The next few weeks were going to be an agony of waiting to confirm the pregnancy and there'd be an even longer wait to see if she carried a dark-haired boy with irresistible Godiva-chocolate eyes.

Toni took the fork in the driveway that led past Granddad's house and parked in the rear. Only company parked out front. With a satisfied sigh she turned off the car. Home, at last.

Matthews, her grandfather's foreman, came out to meet the car. Toni wondered at his weaving gait until he exhaled. The man was drunk at ten o'clock in the morning? Two more hands stumbled out of the bunkhouse, neither looking any more sober.

Their scowls made her feel about as welcome as a swarm of mosquitoes. She summarized her conversation with the lawyer—less a few personal details. "So, I'm moving in."

"We know how things is run round here. Don't you fret yer little head about it, girlie. Me an' the boys'll handle it. Jus' like we been doing since the old man dropped dead."

Toni flinched at the foreman's callous remark. "Would you help me unload the trailer?"

Matthews spit out a wad of chewing tobacco. "We got business to tend to." He turned on his heel and left. The hands followed.

Dumbfounded, Toni stared after them. Things weren't starting out well, but at least she was home. Hefting a box, she lugged it from the tiny U-Haul trailer to the screened back porch. She pulled open the door and propped it with the box. An unclean smell assaulted her.

Beau, the old basset hound her grandfather had given her the summer before she'd gone off to college, rolled off his bed in the corner and lethargically crossed the porch to greet her. Toni dropped to her knees and hugged the dog. His less-than-enthusiastic response concerned her. He usually greeted her with an eardrum-splitting howl.

"Beau? What's the matter, boy? Aren't you glad to see me?" Toni stroked his head then studied his dull brown eyes and dry nose. His ribs showed through his coat. "Beau?"

The dog tried to bark, but only a scratchy sound emerged. Toni glanced at his food and water bowls. Both were empty. Judging by the condition of the back porch the men hadn't let Beau out often enough. She clenched her jaw.

"Are you thirsty?" The black tail thumped once. "Hungry?" The tail tweaked again. "Well, let's see what we can find."

Stepping into the kitchen was like coming home. After filling the dog's bowls, Toni stood back and watched Beau lap the water as if he hadn't had any in days. Anger spiraled inside her. The lawyer had assured her the hands would take care of things. Toni felt another flash of anger over such cruelty.

By the time she'd finished cleaning the porch and unpacking her trailer, she was too tired to study the ranch journals. The stress of the day and two nearly sleepless nights had caught up with her. Exhausted, Toni crawled between the sheets of the bed she'd used since childhood. And dreamed anything but childish dreams about a dark-haired cowboy.

Toni sprang out of bed, looking forward to her first day in charge of the Rocking A. After hustling through breakfast, she rushed out the back door. A much happier and healthier Beau greeted her with a howl and a swinging tail.

"You look better today, boy." He'd damned well better. She'd have shot someone if Beau hadn't responded to the TLC she'd given him yesterday. "Feel like a walk?"

Beau woofed and followed Toni on her survey of the property. In the bright sunlight everything looked faded, run-down. Yesterday she'd been so thrilled to be here she hadn't noticed the disrepair of the buildings. "Oh, Granddad," she moaned.

The sense of loss overwhelmed her. Toni sank down on a bale of hay and let the tears go. She missed coffee on the back porch with Gramps. Missed hearing him hand out orders to the crew from the stoop. Missed the challenge of tagging along and trying not to get caught. The corner of her mouth turned up. He'd always insisted she stay in the compound surrounding the house and outbuildings, but Toni had loved the open spaces. She'd tailed him like a faithful Indian scout.

With her crew nowhere to be found, Toni and Beau headed for the barn. She greeted and fed one horse, then another. The horses had been neglected almost as badly as the dog. They needed a farrier and a vet. She'd call the farrier to tend the hooves. With Granddad's journals and her veterinary training, she didn't doubt for one moment that she could run this ranch, and she was eager to get started. Whistling for Beau, she jogged back to the house to go over the books.

Hours later Toni slumped in the leather office chair. The books looked bad. The ranch didn't have a mortgage, but the amount of cash in the account was pitifully small. There'd be no income from selling cattle for months. She pulled the calculator forward and went through the records once more, figuring her monthly expenses and hoping she'd miscalculated.

Brand climbed into his truck. It had taken a long, frustrating week for the P.I. to get two names and addresses in his hands. He'd filled the time by giving interviews and shooting ads for his sponsors, but his mind wasn't on his work. His thoughts were with the woman who'd made him forget his number-one rule. Don't fool around on the road. And his second rule. If you're stupid enough to fool around, don't do it without taking precautions.

He read the slip of paper in his hand. Antonia Allison Swenson had an apartment near the A & M campus, but the address she'd used at the hotel belonged to a Will Anderson, recently deceased, of the Rocking A Ranch in Texas. Brand started the engine then drummed his fingers on the steering wheel. Where would she be? Her apartment or the Rocking A? He headed south. Arizona and New Mexico blew by in a blur of traffic and hastily eaten truck-stop meals.

What had Toni wanted from him? he asked himself again. She didn't have the look or the experience of a buckle bunny who wanted to start sleeping with cowboys for no other reason than to add another notch to her lipstick case. To be rid of her virginity? Nah, there'd been genuine hunger in her eyes and in her touch. He wasn't bragging to admit that much. *So what did she want?* It irritated him that he hadn't figured it out by the time he crossed the Texas state line. He pulled into a fast-food place, hoping caffeine and food would fuel his brain.

Had she been as caught up in their lovemaking as he'd been and simply forgotten to use protection the last time? Or did she want to get pregnant? The thought exploded into his head with the subtlety of a grenade. She wouldn't be the first female to try that trick, but it didn't make sense. If she'd wanted to get pregnant why pick on a kid like Bobby Lee?

It hit Brand like a sucker punch that he'd been second choice. She'd wanted Bobby Lee, but she'd settled for him. His ego staggered. He tossed his half-eaten burger into the trash. "Why are you so determined to find a woman who used and ditched you, fool?"

Because she might be pregnant, you irresponsible idiot.

He'd never been careless before, and didn't aim to start now. Not when he was so close to his dream of getting out of this career he hadn't wanted and into one he did. His heart wasn't in the rodeo. Never had been. Gold buckle or no, he'd considered making this his last year of competition. He was sick of living out of a suitcase. Tired of having no place to call home. Crooked Creek, the family ranch, didn't count. There, he was no more than an unpaid hand. He did what he was told and had no say in the operation. His father and his oldest brother, Caleb, made all the decisions. He needed more than that.

But he'd be damned if there'd be a little Lander wandering around that he didn't know about. He'd seen it happen to his buddies. A cowboy rode into town, celebrated with a lady and lit out for the next rodeo. Sooner or later, the guy got a registered letter demanding child support or a female demanding a golden ring. It had happened to his older brother and to a few of his friends, but it wasn't going to happen to him. He didn't aim to give it all away because of one foolish night.

It had been one hell of a night. His groin throbbed with remembered passion. Good night or not, if he'd made a kid he was responsible for it. No kid of his would be dumped like garbage.

Muttering a chorus of cuss words, he pulled the truck back onto the highway. The Rocking A Ranch was on his way home. He'd stop and see if Toni was staying at her grandfather's place. If she wasn't, he'd head on to her apartment. On second thoughts, he'd call. Pulling off the highway at the next exit, Brand located a pay phone and got information to dial the number to her apartment.

"The number you have dialed has been disconnected."

Brand slammed the phone into the cradle and dialed up the Rocking A. No answer. Damn. He hoped like hell she was on the Rocking A or, at least, that somebody there knew where to find her. If not, the P.I. was going to get another chunk of his winnings—the part he'd set aside for one particular bull he was itching to buy.

Toni returned from putting fresh flowers on her grandparents' graves. Generations of Andersons had lived on this land and been laid to rest in the family cemetery. Unless fate was on her side, Grandpa Will could be the last. She stopped abruptly at the sight of the three men loitering in the yard. Obviously, they had no intention of following the instructions she'd handed out this morning. "Is there a problem with fixing the fence in the east pasture?"

Matthews wiped his red nose and pursed his lips around a toothpick. Toni smelled alcohol on his breath again. Either he hadn't sobered up from last night, or the man started drinking at sunrise. She was beginning to believe the latter.

"Nope, but I figure we'll work in the west today. Probably be shifting the herd thataway in a day or two anyhow."

Toni shoved her fists in her pockets and ground her teeth. The man's open defiance this past week had driven her pretty darn close to firing him. If she did, she knew the other hands would follow. She couldn't run the place by herself, so she bit her tongue, then repeated her orders. "As I explained this morning, the west pasture needs reseeding. We'll move the cattle to the east pasture next week after they've been inoculated."

All three of them stared at her as if she hadn't spoken English, then turned toward their horses. Impotent fury made Toni stomp her foot. "I want that fence fixed today, Matthews."

Without acknowledging her orders, the men mounted up and turned their horses west. They hadn't gone more than a few yards when a voice stopped them.

"She said east. You need a compass?"

Toni spun toward the whiskey-rough voice. Her hand fluttered to her throat. Her heart stuttered to a stop, then raced in panic. The heat of humiliation fired her face. She'd stolen from the man and then sneaked off like a rustler in the night. She blinked, hoping this was another one of those dreams that had haunted her nights for the past week, but when she opened her eyes, her one-night cowboy was heading her way.

Brand wore black jeans again, but this time a black-and-teal shirt stretched across the breadth of his chest. A large belt buckle winked in the sun with every long stride that covered the yard. He showed no trace of the injury that had turned his knee black and blue. The unwanted memory of how she'd bathed his bruises with her tongue bloomed in Toni's mind.

She tried to speak, but couldn't. She had no idea what

she'd say anyway. He'd found her. She had no contingency plan for that.

Tipping back his hat with a lean finger, he said, "Hello, darlin'. Miss me?"

Some corner of her mind registered the men muttering about Brand's championship belt buckle, but the majority of her synapses focused on the angry golden sparkles in Brand's eyes and the sarcastic edge to his voice.

His clenched jaw didn't look as if it had seen a razor in days, and he didn't look pleased to see her.

He knew what she'd done.

The knowledge chilled her. How would he react? Would she have to physically defend herself? It wasn't likely that she could count on the clowns behind her to help. She remembered the strength in Brand's thickly muscled arms and her stomach knotted with fear.

A mournful howl came from the back porch. Brand looked away, giving her a chance to gather her thoughts. Toni welcomed the distraction. While Beau approached cautiously to sniff out the visitor, Toni considered her options. Running wasn't one of them, but she didn't know the limits of Brand's anger or how far he'd go to punish someone who'd crossed him.

"Hey, you're the one that just won the finals, ain't ya? What brings you out here? You looking to buy this ranch?"

Brand let the dog sniff and lick his hand before straightening to face the men. "That's between her and me. Now I'd suggest you mend the fence in the east pasture like she said."

Matthews's face darkened and his lips compressed, but he kept his objections to himself. He turned his horse toward the eastern pasture. The men followed.

Toni didn't know whether to be thankful for Brand's help or panicked because he'd tracked her down. Panicked, she decided, because if the hard glint in his eyes was anything to go by, this wasn't going to be pleasant. She wiped her palms on her jeans and swallowed the lump in her throat. "Why are you here?"

He looked her up and down, as if searching out her secret. "We have unfinished business."

Beau parked himself between them, his tail thumping in welcome. Her dog had betrayed her and she couldn't blame him. What she'd done was despicable. Toni studied the man she'd wronged and wondered if he'd understand her motives. When the sun hit his face she noticed he looked drawn and paler than she remembered. His lips, the ones that had caressed every inch of her body, were set in a hard line.

Her heart fluttered in fear. "Come inside."

Brand stepped around the droopy basset hound to follow Toni toward the house. He'd seen her naked, but until now, he'd never seen her butt in a pair of jeans. She had a first-class behind. He turned away from the tempting sight and yanked his ear. His hormones were leading him astray when he needed to hold on to his anger.

The house, like the outbuildings, needed repairs. Beneath one of the sheds sat a tractor with a good portion of its parts spread on the ground beneath its belly. Brand pulled the door of the screened porch open for Toni. It gave an ungodly screech worthy of a horror flick. The dog waddled through and settled with an almighty sigh on a pillow in the corner. Brand was tempted to swipe the scattered bits of tack and the jar of saddle soap from the faded cushions of the old wicker sofa and sleep for a week. Exhaustion pulled at him after countless nights of worrying over this mess he'd gotten himself into. He stepped inside the house. Although it looked clean, it wasn't in much better shape than the outside.

"Sit down." Toni pointed toward the scarred wooden table.

Just ask her and leave. It wouldn't take two minutes to clear this mess up then he could hit the road. Brand removed his hat, hooked it on the rack just inside the door, and sat down. He ran a hand through his hair, suddenly nervous for some damn fool reason. Then he noticed the tired droop of Toni's shoulders and the downward curve of her lips. She looked as ragged as he felt.

She brought him a cup of coffee then perched on the edge of a chair. A second later she jumped back up and paced to the window where she hovered like a hummingbird.

"Why are you here?" Toni asked again as she wrung a dish towel in her hands. Brand could see tension and fear in her eyes, but he couldn't afford to be sympathetic.

"Are you pregnant?" His words came out harshly, baldly, as an accusation. Dammit, he'd meant to lead up to the question with a little more finesse, find out why she'd chosen him.

She flinched and paled, leaning back against the window frame as if she'd fall down without its support. Her eyes shifted away, then back. The hairs on the back of Brand's neck stood up.

"I don't know yet," she whispered. Glancing away again, she bit her lip.

Her words hit him like a blow. Whatever he'd expected to hear, he wasn't prepared for that. He'd expected her to laugh, to tell him he'd been fretting over nothing, that she was on the pill, anything but *that*. "Did you plan it?"

He sucked a slow breath, hoping—praying—she'd deny it. Seconds ticked past, each one like another nail in the coffin holding his dreams. *Deny it*, he pleaded silently.

She stared at the floor then slowly lifted her head. "Yes."

Air gushed from his chest, like blood from an arterial wound. *She was trying to trap him.*

"Why me?" It hurt his throat to say the words. Hell, he ought to give her credit for honesty, but anger at her and disappointment in himself nearly choked him. God help him, he'd thought her different from the other women who used a man for sport. How wrong could he be? Hadn't he learned anything about the true nature of women from his mother and ex-sister-in-law? They wanted to be kept, given a free ride, and they'd lied, cheated and stolen to get it.

He'd thought he was smart enough not to fall into the trap.

She twisted the towel, then tossed it down and squared her shoulders. "Look, I'm sorry for involving you. It wasn't... personal."

His mouth dropped open. He slammed his cup to the table and jumped to his feet, ignoring what looked like fear in her eyes. "Not personal! Lady, I was *inside you* and I'm the only man who's ever been there. That's pretty damned personal."

She held her hands up and backed away a few steps. "I guess I just didn't think it through. I never expected a guy would care as long as I didn't ask for support or anything. I'll sign a paper waiving you of any parental obligations." She turned her head away, but he could still see the blush on her cheek.

"The whole point of going to bed with a stranger...was that he—*you*—weren't supposed to know if there were consequences. And you don't have to know, Brand. Go. Leave. Drive away."

"Not until I know for sure." *And then what will you do, sucker?* Damned if he knew. Other than his little brother, he hadn't been around kids much, didn't even know if he liked 'em. But without a doubt he wouldn't abandon any child of his, not after the way he'd been raised.

He needed time to think, time to plan his next move. No matter what she said he wasn't about to leave. He searched for a safer topic while his mind scrambled for answers. "Your foreman always give you that much trouble?"

The vibrant, feisty angel he'd made love—had sex with—he corrected, had wilted. Toni shifted uneasily, looking fragile enough to break in a gentle breeze. *No sympathy, dammit. The woman has robbed you.*

Toni sighed and wiped a trembling hand across her pale forehead. "Yeah."

The tenderness he felt over her vulnerability angered him. It was probably an act.

"Sit down before you fall down." Brand pulled out a chair. After a moment's hesitation, Toni collapsed into it. He crossed to the draining rack and picked up a mug. Filling it with the fragrant coffee, he set it on the table and straddled a chair in front of her. "Why were you trying to get pregnant?"

Toni straightened her spine. Her color came back in a rush. "It's none of your business."

Brand leaned forward. "If it's my kid, it sure as hell is my business." She flinched and he realized he'd yelled. He made an effort to soften his voice. "I'm not leaving, so start talking."

Her chin lifted to a challenging angle. He expected her to tell him to go to hell any minute, but her gaze fell. He thought she might be pouting, until he saw her chin wobble. "My grandfather died."

His heart twisted at the pain in her voice. *No sympathy.* "Yeah, I know. Sorry."

Her head jerked up. "How—"

"I hired a private detective to track you." He could tell by the tightening of her lips and the way she strangled her cup that she didn't like that tidbit. "What's that got to do with what happened in Vegas?"

Again she studied the coffee as if the answers to all her problems resided in the dark brew. "He wouldn't leave the ranch to me. I'm female."

"I noticed." Sparks shot from her eyes at his sarcasm.

"He didn't believe a woman has any place on a ranch. At least not outside the house. He was…protective." She shoved her mug away and fisted her hands on the table. Small, delicate hands, but strong. She'd clenched them in his hair and held him to her breasts. Those slender, short-nailed fingers had dug into his buttocks, raked across his chest and back. A flash of heat ricocheted through him. Brand shot to his feet and paced to the window.

"Granddad wasn't just chauvinistic. He honestly didn't believe I could handle the responsibility of a ranch alone. I'm a vet, for crying out loud, but he didn't think I could manage the herd. Stick to puppies and kitties, he said."

Brand turned with a jerk. Perhaps his angel wasn't the bit of fluff he'd believed. "You're a veterinarian?"

"Yeah. I graduated this past summer. I'd talked to Grandpa before he died, but he never mentioned his plans for the place or I'd have…" She shook her head and gave a dispirited sigh and rubbed her temple. "I have to produce a husband or a male child within the year or the property will be sold."

Her crazy plan was starting to make sense. Brand's gaze dropped to her flat stomach. The mere thought of his child growing inside her made it difficult for him to breathe. "What happens if you're not pregnant or if you have a girl?"

Toni's hands trembled until she clasped them tightly around her mug. "Plan B. I'll hire a temporary husband."

Her words lit the fuse of his anger, but at least she wasn't talking about getting rid of the kid if it was female. "Is this place worth it? You're sacrificing an innocent baby and selling yourself to get your hands on a chunk of dirt and a few run-down buildings. Let me guess, I'd be getting a call in about nine months."

She shot to her feet and glared. The surge of red into her pale cheeks made her look closer to spitting mad than passing out like she had a minute ago. He shouldn't have cared.

"You made your feelings clear in Vegas. I would never call you, Brand. You don't want to be married. Well, neither do I, but I listened to my grandfather spin yarns about this place for as long as I can remember. I know how prosperous it once was and it will be again." She jerked her thumb to her chest. "With me at the helm.

"As for the child…" Her face and voice softened. "Boy or girl, I'd love it and do my best for it. How could I do any less?" She rubbed her temple as if fighting off a headache. "But life would sure be easier if it were a boy."

Brand noted the tears in her eyes before she blinked them away. He reluctantly gave her points for not turning on the waterworks. His mother had been a master at that.

"Toni, the place is falling apart. From what I saw, most of the buildings need structural repairs, and the fences look like they'll fall with the first strong breeze. You have boards and roofing that need replacing and everything needs a coat of paint. Do you have the cash for that?"

She crumpled into her chair and put her head in her hands. Her hair fell forward to reveal the tender nape of her neck. Brand had to jerk himself back to the matter at hand.

"I barely have enough to make payroll for the next few months. I can't fire that good-for-nothing crew because they're cheap. To get better help, I'd have to pay better wages, and I just don't have…" She bit her lip, looking as if she regretted telling him her problem. "Maybe when I've sold some cattle…"

"You're talking a hell of a lot of money, Toni. More than a few head of cattle will bring. You'd probably have to sell your entire herd to raise that kind of cash. Next year you'll be in the same bind, but you won't have any stock to sell."

Her eyes narrowed on him in appraisal. "You sound like you know ranching."

Brand shrugged. "Grew up on one. What if you're pregnant? How will you work the ranch and raise a baby by yourself?"

She pinched her lips and squared her shoulders. Brand had to admire her grit. Even if she was ignoring the obvious. "I'll manage."

"You need a partner with capital." He watched her weigh the idea, then her chin jutted out in what was already becoming a familiar gesture. Seconds ticked past. He couldn't blame her for wanting to hold on to the place. The buildings might need work, but from what he'd seen driving in, the land looked good. Judging by the number of fence posts he'd passed, it was a pretty good-size spread.

Resignation settled over Toni's features. "Maybe a silent partner."

Brand frowned and stroked his brow. She'd skipped town, trying to steal his child from him once already. Would she do it again? No doubt about it. There was only one way he could guarantee himself legal rights to his child if she decided to bolt.

Marry her.

"Fifty-fifty. Your ranch. My money." He heard the words leave his mouth and wondered if he'd lost his freakin' mind. He'd always sworn he'd never tie himself to a woman. They demanded too much and were never happy. His father and brother had nearly killed themselves trying to keep their wives happy and what had happened? The women had left anyway, but not until the money had run out.

Toni looked as if she, too, doubted his sanity. He hadn't thought it possible for her eyes to get any bluer, her skin to get any paler. He'd been wrong. Her hand fluttered to her throat, but not before he saw her pulse pounding there. "What if I'm not pregnant?"

Hell, at least he'd get her back into his bed for however long the marriage lasted. For some reason Toni Swenson got to him in a way no other woman had. Might as well figure out why. He shrugged. "You said you'd inherit if you got married?"

She nodded hesitantly.

"Then, you will. To me."

Her eyes and lips rounded. Her throat worked convulsively. "I...I don't want to get married," she whispered.

"Me neither, darlin', but I'll be damned if you'll take my kid and run off." He didn't need to add *again*.

The cornered look was back on her face. She paced toward the door and back a couple of times, stopping in front of him with that determined glint in her eyes. "I'd insist on a prenuptial agreement. I'm not losing this place to a man who decides to go off and search for..." she shifted uncomfortably and glanced away "...greener pastures."

Brand leaned against the edge of the counter, crossed his legs at the ankle, and hooked a thumb through his belt loop. So she wanted to make demands, did she? "What makes you think I'd ever find a woman who's better in bed than you?"

He'd shocked her. Well, hell, he'd been trying to. So why did he feel like a jackass? Her pink lips parted. Her eyes widened, and her face turned beet-red. She looked everywhere but at him. Her voice squeaked. "I'd still want a prenup—"

"Fine. It'll take a few days to get the license and for my family to get here. If you can have it drawn up by then, I'll sign it." He curved his finger around her chin and turned her until their eyes met. "Fifty-fifty, Toni. I'll take nothing less."

Her nearness immediately made him start thinking of things he shouldn't be thinking. Brand straightened and put some space between them. "One more thing. When you leave, I get sole custody of the child—if there is one—and first right of refusal on your share of this ranch."

"And if you leave?"

Brand nearly snorted. It wasn't the man who cut loose. "Same deal."

Toni's knees felt rubbery, and she had to clench the counter for support. How had all her meticulous planning backfired? And why would Brand make such ridiculous demands? Didn't he know a mother would never willingly give up her child?

Movement in the backyard drew her attention away from the crazy cowboy she was seriously considering marrying. The ranch hands loitered by the bunkhouse. Her foreman lifted a flask to his lips then passed it to the next man who took a swig and passed it on. Toni sucked an angry breath. Brand stepped behind her. Too close. She could feel his breath on her nape and the heat radiating from his body.

He slammed a fist on the counter and Toni nearly jumped out of her skin. "Cut their checks. I'm going to fire the crew."

"But… What'll I do for help?" She stopped him with a hand on his arm. His muscles clenched beneath her fingers and she jerked her hand away. How could she be considering marrying a man with such powerful arms and big hands?

He leveled his dark eyes on her. "I know plenty of cowboys who need work off-season. Soon as I put the word out we'll have 'em lining up." Brand settled his hat on his head and strode out the back door.

Toni closed her eyes and rubbed her temple. Things were going from bad to worse with the speed of a twister ripping through her life. She stumbled into her grandfather's office and sank into his old leather chair. It smelled of him. Usually, it soothed her to sit here, made her feel safe, but today her fingers still burned from the contact with Brand and her hands shook so badly she could barely write the checks.

She laid the pen down and buried her face in her hands. What had she done? Had she made a bargain with the devil? She could already be pregnant with a stranger's child. She touched her belly. She didn't know how to be a mother. She'd never even been a baby-sitter. Now, she'd agreed to become a wife to a man she didn't know other than in the biblical sense. A big man. A physical man.

Tying herself to him terrified her, but there wasn't another option. Her gaze fell on the letter beside the blotter. The bank had refused her loan request. Toni looked at the last entry in her grandfather's journal. Two of the wells had run dry and the barn roof leaked like a sieve. He'd been worried that the first big rain could destroy all the feed stored under a tarp in the loft.

The unexpected expenses she dreaded were already adding up. Worse, if she'd counted the herd correctly, her grandfather had been running fewer cattle than he should have been for a ranch this size. Brand was right—there wouldn't be enough money for all the repairs if she sold every steer and every piece of equipment on the place.

Being a qualified vet was fine and dandy, but if she didn't have the money to buy the supplies she needed she couldn't care for the animals. Add in feed costs, salaries, her college-loan payment, and the day-to-day operating expenses and the result was a negative number. She wouldn't ask her parents for the money. There would be strings. Her father always had strings.

She had to take Brand on as a partner. And as a husband. But how could she be sure he wouldn't try to take the place from her? How could she be sure he wouldn't hurt her? Toni stiffened her spine. She could protect herself and her baby, and she'd have her grandfather's attorney draw up an airtight legal document to protect her land. Losing this ranch to some itinerant rodeo bum was not an option. As for his thinking she'd leave and he'd get custody of her child...

Well, *she* wouldn't be the one leaving.

Four

Brand surveyed the buildings with a critical eye as he crossed the yard, making a mental list of supplies he'd need and the amount of time and labor the work would require. It was a long list. Nearly as long as the list of reasons why he shouldn't be marrying Toni, and he had to be plumb loco even to consider it. Still, he'd do it and take on the challenge of getting this ranch back into prime condition—if for no other reason than the kid she might be carrying.

His kid.

Brand stopped in front of the foreman. The hands picked at their tack, trying to look busy. ''You have trouble finding the east pasture?''

''Nah. We'll move the herd in a few days. There's no need to waste time on that fence right now. That li'l girl don't know squat 'bout cattle.''

''You disobeyed a direct order. Pack your gear. You're fired.''

"You can't fire me, boy." The foreman puffed up his chest and advanced.

Brand planted his feet and watched the drunk. He was used to men who threw their weight around. "Clear out."

"Me an' Will had an agreement. I'm staying."

"Nope, you're going."

He'd expected the punch. Brand caught the meaty fist, twisted it and had the foreman flat on his back in the dirt. The other men either weren't drunk enough to fight him, or they had better sense. Disgusted, Brand headed for the house. He heard a grunt and turned. The foreman shot to his feet. Fast and agile for a man of his girth and alcohol content, he caught Brand in a chest-crushing squeeze, pinning his arms to his sides. "Let's teach this here bull rider a lesson, boys."

The other two men clenched their fists and approached. Before he could curse his stupidity for turning his back on the man, Brand heard a *crack-ping*. The metal tractor sign on a light pole above their heads rocked. There was a bullet hole dead center on the tractor tire in the picture. He yanked his gaze toward the house.

Toni stood on the back steps, staring down the sight of the rifle propped on her shoulder. She pointed it straight at the foreman. "Pack and leave. The sheriff's on his way."

The arms bruising Brand's ribs dropped and the foreman stepped away, muttering a few ripe words. The men hustled into the bunkhouse as she crossed the yard.

"I don't like this," she said, putting the safety on the rifle. Brand noticed the trembling of her voice and the white line around her lips. The confrontation had definitely spooked her. "He might make trouble."

"I'll take care of it."

"Excuse me?" she protested huffily. The look in Toni's eyes reminded Brand of the way she'd looked at the rodeo. Determined.

"We'll keep an eye out." Brand noted the competent

way she handled the weapon. "You're going to have to tell me your secrets, darlin'."

She eyed him warily.

"The marksmanship." How many other secrets did she have?

A sheriff's car pulled off the highway and headed up the dirt driveway with enough speed to throw a rooster tail of dust in its wake. It slid to a halt a few feet away. A young man flung the door open and climbed out. "I had a call about a disturb— Toni?"

"Josh?"

His brand-new fiancée dashed across the yard to hug a man who looked more like a landlocked surfer than a deputy. The burn in Brand's gut had nothing to do with jealousy—he hadn't known Toni long enough for that, and he damn sure wasn't ever going to like her enough to be jealous. The woman was not to be trusted.

The deputy sheriff glanced from the rifle tucked under Toni's arm to Brand. His hand settled on the butt of his pistol. "This man giving you trouble?"

"Brand? No. He…I…we…"

"I'm Brand Lander, Toni's fiancé." Brand stepped forward, stuck out his right hand, and snaked his left around Toni's waist, pulling her against his side.

"Josh Keegan." The deputy hesitated then shook Brand's hand. Toni looked less than happy about the situation. She held herself stiffly against him—a far cry from the way she'd melted all over him in Vegas. Her gaze darted between him and the deputy.

"So what's the disturbance?"

"We're firing some hands. They're not in a hurry to leave," Toni told him.

"You mean your grandfather left the place to you after all? I can't believe the old coot finally relented. He forget you're a girl?"

"Not exactly." Toni squirmed, but Brand refused to let

her go. "Josh, I'm worried that my ex-foreman, Matthews, might cause trouble. He already tried to hurt Brand."

"Pressing charges?" Keegan flipped open his notepad.

"Not this time. Just noted," Brand answered.

Nodding, Josh jotted the details down as Brand gave them. "Wouldn't be the first time your foreman's been in trouble. He gets into a bar fight in town at least once a month."

The men came out of the bunkhouse, tossed their gear in the back of a pickup truck and peeled out of the driveway. Keegan took down the license-plate number and the men's names. Business completed, he studied Toni again as if she were the best thing since homemade ice cream. Brand didn't like it.

"It's great to see you. What've you been doing?"

She smiled at the lawman in a way she'd never smiled at Brand. He didn't like that, either. As a matter of fact, Brand decided, he didn't like one damn thing about Deputy Keegan. Not his pretty-boy face. Not his friendly attitude. Especially not the way he eyed Toni. Territorial was something he'd never been before.

It's because she might be carrying my kid.

"I finished vet school. You want to come in for coffee, Josh?"

Brand glared at the lawman. "I'm sure the deputy needs to get back on patrol, darlin'."

Josh shot Brand a cautious glance and backed toward his patrol car. "Well…uh…I really should be going. I'll stop by another time and take you up on that invitation, Toni."

The car disappeared in a cloud of dust. Toni stepped away.

"How dare you be so rude to Josh." Despite her bold words, Brand thought she watched him warily. She stood on the balls of her feet as if ready to move fast or dodge. He frowned.

"The deal goes both ways. I don't cheat. You don't cheat."

She practically sputtered with anger. "For Pete's sake, Josh is like a brother to me."

"Tell him that. Did your grandfather pay his foreman enough for him to be able to buy a thirty-thousand-dollar truck?"

The fire in Toni's eyes turned to suspicion. Her brow puckered. "I don't think so."

"There's a lot that needs to be done here. Let me tell you where I want to start." Brand headed toward one of the barns.

Toni parked her hands on her hips and ground her teeth. "Listen, Lander, this is supposed to be a partnership, not a dictatorship. If this is going to work we need to discuss expenses beforehand."

Toni had a feeling the battle lines had just been drawn in the dust beneath her feet. Brand stopped abruptly and slowly turned. One hand fisted, the other shifted his hat. "Would you care to show me around so we can discuss the repairs? I have a few suggestions."

His words dripped sarcasm and his eyes held the warmth of a polar ice cap. She rubbed her forehead and the doozy of a headache announcing its presence in her brow. Battling wills with a hardheaded cowboy wouldn't improve it any—especially not when he was angry. There was no doubt in her mind that Brand Lander was powerful. More powerful than her father. She'd seen his strength when he'd stopped Matthews's punch.

Keep your distance. Use reason. Reason sometimes works.

She inched cautiously toward him. "More important than the outbuildings are the two dry wells, the downed fences, and the pastures that need reseeding. We can't increase or maintain the herd without those."

Surprise flashed in Brand's eyes. He nodded to acknowledge her point. "Can we take the truck or do we need to saddle up?"

Toni waved toward the old truck parked in the side yard. "We can drive, if we can get a vehicle running. My car won't make it through the fields."

"I'll look at the truck later. We can take mine."

Toni followed Brand around the front of the house. A white king-cab truck sat beneath the oak tree. Brand held open the door, and Toni climbed in. "This isn't exactly the overloaded boy toy I'd expect a four-time world champion to drive."

Bracing his arms on the door opening, Brand said, "I need a reliable ride to get from one rodeo to the next—not a chick magnet. I bought this truck and another one for my dad with my first big check. The majority of my winnings, I've put in the bank or invested."

His calluses scraped gently along her jaw. Toni caught her breath as awareness arched between them. Brand lowered his head.

Toni leaned back. "Don't."

"Don't?"

"I'll marry you, but I'm not—I'm not sleeping with you."

Brand stepped back, frowning. "I don't remember you saying no in Vegas."

She didn't want to say no now. "We hardly know each other."

"We were good, Toni. Better than good."

"I know, but…I need time."

"How much time?"

"I—I don't know. I don't love you and I—" She'd never expected to enjoy making love with a man she didn't love.

"It wasn't love you wanted that night. Hell, it wasn't even *me* you wanted. You wanted Bobby Lee."

She'd stung his pride. "No, no, I didn't want Bobby

Lee. I wanted a cowboy who wouldn't follow me home. He seemed the type. You on the other hand..." She shrugged. No need to state the obvious.

"Don't mention the baby to my family," Brand said the following day without looking up from the supply list on the table in front of him.

Coffee splashed over the rim of Toni's cup, burning her fingers. She snatched them back. "Brand, I may not be pregnant. It was just one night."

One long, passionate night. Toni blew on her stinging fingers and concentrated on regulating her breathing. She'd spent the morning pretending Brand didn't look fabulous in his tight jeans and his brightly patterned shirt. Attraction would cloud the issue. A clear head was crucial.

Brand was beside her in two strides, examining her hand then thrusting it under cold running water. Toni jerked away. "I'm okay."

Grabbing the plate of pancakes he'd left for her on the stove, she sat at the far end of the table. Not that she expected to eat. She was too nervous. It was her wedding day. "It's not like I'm going to greet your family with 'Nice to meet you, I might be pregnant.' So tell me why you felt the need to warn me."

Brand sat down and focused on the paper in front of him. The sun shining in through the window glistened on his hair and lit the tiny nick on his clean-shaven jaw. Darn the man for looking good first thing in the morning when she felt about as energetic as a wet mop after tossing and turning all night.

"My brother Caleb was trapped into marriage by a woman claiming to be carrying his child. Not only was the baby a piece of fiction, his marriage was two years of hell for all of us."

Toni set down her fork and tried to ease the lump in her throat. She was marrying a stranger and acquiring his family—a family that was likely to hate her when they found out what she'd done. "What other land mines do I need to avoid?"

Brand drummed his fingers on the table. Toni thought he wasn't going to answer. His usually sensuous lips looked as tight as his shoulders. "Let's just say my family shares your grandfather's opinion that a woman doesn't belong on a ranch."

"I'm perfectly capable—" Anger choked off her words. Were all men this sexist? Toni slammed her cup down on the table. "What is wrong with a woman running a ranch?"

Something in the depths of Brand's eyes dried up her arguments. He blinked and the look was gone. "My mother split when I was eight. Guess she got sick of being stuck in the house all day with sniveling brats."

Bitterness and hurt hardened his voice and twisted his lips. Toni's heart ached for the lost little boy he must have been. "I guess I'm not going to be welcomed with open arms."

He snorted. "Hardly."

Appetite gone, she shoved her plate aside. "Why'd you leave home?"

Brand crossed the room to put his dishes in the sink. "I was tired of busting my butt and not having any say in the ranch. There were a lot of things Dad could've done different, but he wasn't willing to change or to listen to a smart-mouthed kid's ideas." He clenched his fist and stared out the window. "And then there was the rodeo."

Toni had a feeling there was more to it than that, but he obviously didn't want to share. "Tell me about the rest of your family. How many brothers?"

Brand rinsed his mug. "Three. Caleb's ten years older. Patrick, eight. Cort is six years younger than me." His tone and face softened. "He's in medical school at Duke."

"Oh my gosh, he was only two when your mother left."

Brand shoved his hat on his head and turned toward the door. "I have things to do. Ring the bell if I'm not back when they get here. Your turn to cook breakfast tomorrow.''

He snatched up a leftover sausage link and carried it out the door. Beau, the traitor, waited, his tail thumping.

Brand saddled up the most ornery mount in the barn, a young sorrel gelding with more buck than brains. Trying to stay on the back of a horse determined to feed him dirt ought to keep his mind occupied. Wrong. His mother's voice rang through his head as clear as if she'd left yesterday. He remembered sitting on her bed, an unwilling confidant, watching her pack. Cort had been crying in his crib in the next room.

"I have to go, Brandon. I'd sooner put a gun to my head than stay. Your dad, Caleb and Patrick will take care of the ranch. You take care of Cort. That's your job. I can't do it anymore. When things settle down, I'll come for you and Cort.''

He'd been eight years old. It had taken a while, but he'd figured it out. When the going got tough, the women got going. There was nothing like the emptiness he'd felt standing on the porch juggling his squirming and screaming two-year-old brother and watching his mother drive out of sight. She hadn't come back.

Sooner or later, kid or no kid, Toni would bail out, and, like his dad, he'd be left to struggle with the land and his kid. The difference was that he wouldn't need to work his kids like slaves to make a living. He could afford to hire help. The Rocking A was a fine piece of land to raise a kid on. Whenever Toni decided to leave, he'd offer her a fair price.

Between now and then he wasn't going to make the mistake his dad and brother had of falling in love with the women they married and getting his heart ripped out.

Toni smoothed her hand down the fitted bodice of the wedding dress Brand had bought her and opened the door to three big, sour-faced men. All had the same dark hair and eyes as Brand, but none had his easy smile or his lean build. Somber in their Sunday best and slicked-down hair, they looked better suited to attending a funeral than a wedding.

"Hello, I'm Toni Swenson." Her voice came out a little weak. To compensate, she plastered on a big, fake smile and extended her hand toward the oldest man.

He sized her up before he took her hand in a meaty grip. Judging by his scowl, she hadn't fared well. "Jack Lander. My sons, Caleb, Patrick and... Where the hell is the boy?"

"Over here." A younger man straightened from petting Beau and headed her way. "I'm Cort. You must be Toni. Damn, Brand's got good taste. Ditch him and run away with me, darlin'." He winked and Toni had to laugh. Cort had Brand's smile and charm, albeit a less potent version.

"Stuff it, brat." Brand said behind her. The hair on her neck immediately rose. He snaked an arm around her waist and reached past her to give Cort a playful noogie.

Toni wondered if Brand planned to pretend this was a love match. She eased away from his scorching grip and glanced his way for a clue. Her mouth dropped open. In a dark suit Brand was positively breathtaking. The Western-cut jacket emphasized the breadth of his shoulders, while the white banded-collar shirt accentuated his tan.

The phone rang and Brand said, "I'll get it. I'm expecting a call."

Toni eyed the men. An uneasy silence settled over them. With the exclusion of Cort, the Lander men studied her as if she were a new and fatal strain of virus. "Come in. I'll uh...make coffee."

Caleb Lander scowled at her. "You knocked up?"

She nearly tripped over the hem of her dress. The rest of the family didn't appear to be surprised by his rudeness. No doubt their hasty marriage had been speculated over. "I—"

Brand scowled as he reentered the room. "That's no way to greet my fiancée."

"Just looking out for you, little brother."

"I can look out for myself."

Turning to Toni, Brand put his hands on her shoulders and squeezed. "Did I mention you look beautiful?"

His thumbs circled at the base of her neck, smoothing out the knots of tension. The man had magical hands. Toni would have purred if she hadn't been nervous enough to throw up.

Luckily, his brother broke the spell.

Cort pulled a check from his pocket. "Brand, you sent too much money in the tuition check again."

"Keep it. I don't want you working *and* going to school."

"It's just more that I'll have to pay you back," Cort argued. "I can get financial aid—"

"I don't want the money. Let's go."

Toni's stomach lurched, her heart beat erratically and her knees refused to work. She thought she might pass out. Brand pulled her from her chair. She flinched when she saw his hand coming toward her face, but all he did was tip her chin with a calloused finger.

"You all right?" The concern in his eyes looked genuine, but he could have been acting for his family's benefit. After all, he *had* bought her this exquisite gown. Swallowing her nausea, she nodded and let him propel her out the door. The long full skirt of her satin wedding dress blew in the breeze.

Brand suspected that meeting his family wasn't easy for Toni. Her skin was magnolia pale—almost as pale as her dress—and she acted more skittish than a new filly. He probably shouldn't have bought something so low-cut that he'd be distracted by the curves of her breasts, but the dress had reminded him of the black thing she'd worn in Vegas. It looked virginal and sinful at the same time. He opened the truck door for her.

"Can I ride with you?" Cort asked. Brand motioned him to the rear seat before helping Toni get her dress all tucked in. The others followed in the family pickup.

Cort asked a hundred questions about the NFR finals. Brand was thankful for the distraction. He was more nervous than he'd been before he'd mounted his last bull at the finals, and it had nothing to do with the money riding on the deal.

Toni's lawyer had been out of town, but his partner had drawn up the prenuptial agreement. She'd leave him with no more than she came with, and he had first option to buy her out. She'd even put in the custody clause he'd requested. His mouth twisted with bitterness. What kind of woman would sign away her child? *Any kind*, he reminded himself. Women, with few exceptions, were quitters.

He'd decided late last night that he wanted his family to believe they were marrying for love. One day his son or daughter might ask questions. Brand wanted the kid to know that he'd done everything he could to keep Toni around. He'd blamed his father for not finding some way to make his mother stay, and he didn't want his child blaming him for Toni's desertion.

If there is a kid.

Maybe he was jumping the gun by refusing to wait a couple more weeks and find out, but he couldn't risk Toni bolting. Brand shrugged his tight shoulders. It didn't make sense that he was getting superstitious now when he never had been on the circuit—heaven knows bull riders were a superstitious bunch. His gut instinct told him there'd be a baby. He couldn't believe something as earth-shattering as his night with Toni could pass without some visible effect.

"So how'd you guys meet?" Cort asked.

"At a rodeo." Brand glanced at Toni's chalky face. She knew what she wanted and went for it. He was that way himself. It was a little too easy to admire her strength, tenacity and levelheadedness. Hell, she could look at a situation and sum it up in a couple of words while he was still studying the angles. In other circumstances he could like her.

"So, was it love at first sight?"

"What do you think?" Brand answered.

Toni chewed her lip.

"You don't drag your feet when you know what you want."

"Yep." Brand pulled the truck into a parking spot.

Toni came out of whatever trance she'd been in to say, "We need to park closer to the courthouse."

Her pallor combined with the white dress made her blue eyes almost luminescent, and she'd painted her lips with a pale pink. He liked them better bare and didn't resist the impulse to lean across the seat and kiss her lipstick off. It had nothing to do with convincing his family.

Her lips parted beneath his. Need slammed him as hard, if not harder, than it had in Vegas. The woman was as heady as a straight shot of tequila on an empty stomach. He swept his tongue inside her mouth to taste her. The urge to lay the truck seat back and make love to her right here beneath the church steeple surprised him. Releasing the catch of her safety belt, Brand pulled her closer.

"Get a room." Cort laughed and punched his shoulder.

Brand drew back reluctantly and felt a little embarrassed. Toni's flushed face and erratic breathing mirrored his own. She'd turned him into a hormone-driven adolescent. Toni scooted toward her door as if she couldn't get away from him fast enough. He caught her hand. "This the church where your parents married?"

She nodded. "I thought we were having a civil service."

Brand shook his head and got out of the truck. He opened her door. Toni's teeth dug into her bottom lip so hard, he expected to see blood. With his thumb, he rescued her lip from the nip of her teeth. Her cold hands trembled in his. Evidently, she didn't want to do this any more than he did. For some damned reason, that irked him. "Let me get the camera for Cort. He's our photographer today."

Toni headed up the walk.

"So, *is* she pregnant?" Cort asked.

"Won't be for lack of trying if she's not."

"Do you love her?"

Brand's gaze tracked her. No doubt about it, his new wife-to-be had him hooked. But love? Uh-uh. "What do you think?"

"Come on, give me details, or I'm gonna make up my own."

Brand grinned. "You do that."

He followed Toni up the walk. For as long as it lasted, he and Toni would be one hell of a team. In bed and out.

Five

Toni walked toward the church, her nerves knotting tighter with each step.

She had to be crazy. She didn't even know if she was pregnant. But what if she was? Or wasn't? What if she had a precious baby girl instead of the boy she so desperately needed? She had to do this. Marrying Brand would guarantee she wouldn't lose her ranch. Once the estate was probated and the deed was in her name, she and Brand could go their separate ways.

How could she be contemplating *divorce* before the ceremony? Except in extreme cases, like her parents, marriage should be forever. Her throat ached with unshed tears. Another strong conviction bites the dust. First she had sex with a stranger. Now she stood in front of a church wearing an exquisite wedding dress and contemplating divorce.

Brand stopped beside her. The man was absolutely gorgeous. He'd left his hat at home. The light wind ruffled the thick, dark strands and left a curl across his forehead.

Toni twisted her purse strap around her fingers to keep from brushing it back. Gentleness from a man was something she didn't understand. Hatred? Yes. Fear? Certainly. But thus far she had no reason to feel either of those debilitating emotions for Brand.

"How'd you know about the church?"

He shrugged. "Saw the picture of your parents in the living room. I recognized the place when I came to town for the license. The preacher remembers you and your folks."

She could hear the question in his voice, but she didn't want to explain why she hadn't invited her parents. She'd told Brand they couldn't make it and refused to elaborate.

Her eyes stung. She didn't want him to be gentle or kind or thoughtful. She didn't want to know he was paying his brother's tuition or that he'd bought his dad a truck. She wanted Brand to be a macho jerk she could easily resist and forget.

"It's bad enough that you're getting married, but in a church?" Grimacing, Patrick jerked a thumb toward the weathered stone building. "Damnation, Brand, when was the last time you stepped inside one of these for anything but a funeral?"

Brand ignored him, cupped Toni's elbow, and led her into the vestibule.

Mrs. Betts, the preacher's wife, met them inside the door. She hugged Toni, then pressed a bouquet into her hands. "Toni, it's nice to see you on a happy occasion this time. You look lovely, dear."

Toni stared at the flowers. "Mrs. Betts, you didn't have to—"

"Brand asked me to pick them up," the woman interrupted with a wink in Brand's direction. "White roses, you said, but I remembered how much Toni used to love the daisies we planted out front. She used to pick one every Sunday when Will wasn't looking. I hope you don't mind that I asked the florist to add a few to the bouquet."

Brand dipped his head. "Not at all, ma'am."

Surprised, Toni turned to Brand. His lips quirked up in his trademark grin, but his eyes remained serious. "A bride has to have flowers, darlin'."

Her heart did a swan dive. His charm was lethal. She'd had a nearly toxic dose of it and was going down for the count. Was this what had happened to her mother?

"Everything set?" Brand asked.

"We're ready whenever you are." Mrs. Betts beamed. "You have the license?"

Brand handed over the papers and guided Toni into the silent sanctuary with a hand at her waist. Reverend Betts turned to greet them. Toni barely heard what he said. Candlelight, flowers, stained glass. *What was she doing?*

The reverend positioned them at the end of the aisle. Mrs. Betts stood on one side and Brand on her other. Brand's father and brothers stood behind them. *Trapped.* Toni strangled her bouquet until Mrs. Betts pried it from her fingers. Everything seemed to go into slow motion. Brand took her hand in his. The preacher asked for the rings. Toni's heart stuttered. *She hadn't bought a ring.* Cort winked, dug into his pocket and withdrew two wide gold bands. The vows were the ones young girls dream of making, but to Toni it seemed wrong to be saying them when she didn't believe in love and didn't expect to be tied to this man "till death us do part."

Toni tallied her sins. She'd slept with a stranger and deceived him to get pregnant. Now she stood before an altar and lied. She'd go to hell, for sure. Panic put a lump in her throat. She couldn't breathe, couldn't swallow, couldn't speak.

Brand's steady gaze locked with hers. He repeated his vows, his voice deep and even, then he slid the band onto her finger. His hands were steady. Hers shook so much she nearly dropped the ring before she could push it over his scarred knuckle.

"You may kiss your bride, Brand."

He cupped her face and covered her lips, branding her as his. He angled his head and slid his hands down her back, deepening the kiss and pulling her flush against him. Toni lost all sense of time and place. Brand's heart pounded beneath her hand. His scent and taste invaded her bloodstream like a narcotic. She felt the heat of his desire against her belly. An answering warmth flooded hers.

"Jeez, Brand, save it for tonight." Cort's teasing words severed the connection with the cool precision of a new scalpel.

Toni's hand fluttered from Brand's chest to her own. She'd added lusting in church to her sins.

Cort kissed her hot cheek and winked. "I'm telling you, Toni, you shoulda held out for me."

She tried to laugh, but couldn't. She'd tied herself to a man who made his living with his muscles.

The preacher led them into an alcove and passed her a pen. *Antonia Swenson Lander,* she signed. Her stomach felt like the middle of a beehive.

"You'll fax a copy of this to the attorney?" Brand asked Reverend Betts after signing his name.

"He'll have it in five minutes." Reverend Betts passed the marriage license to his wife who bustled off. "You made a lovely bride, dear. You just let me know when we'll need a christening."

Toni darted a startled glance at the clergyman. Brand squeezed her hand. "We'll do that."

Outside the church the clouds had given way to sunshine. Cort rode with his family, leaving Toni and Brand to cover the miles home alone. Her heart hammered with the enormity of what she'd done. She'd never wanted to marry, never wanted to give a man that kind of power over her, and yet the sunlight bouncing off the golden bands on their hands told her she had. Brand had not only saved her ranch, he'd given her the kind of wedding the tight-knit community could accept. "Thank you."

Brand shot her a curious glance. "For what?"

"The dress, the flowers, the church, the pictures. It seems…real."

"This *is* a real marriage, Toni. Don't doubt it." The gleam in his eyes left her in no doubt of his meaning. Her nerve endings sizzled. Her stomach knotted. The truck cab suddenly seemed airless.

"Brand—" Dozens of cars lined the ranch driveway. Only a barn or house fire brought this kind of crowd. Toni threw open the door. "What's going on?"

The Landers' truck and the Bettses' car pulled in behind them. Brand helped Toni down from the cab. Mrs. Betts bustled over and squeezed Toni's hand. "I hope you don't mind, but so many people remember you from your visits to your granddad. We all wanted to welcome you and your groom home. I'm just sorry your mother couldn't make it."

Toni cringed. She hadn't invited her mother because her mother wouldn't come alone, and there was no way to predict how her father would react. It was best to put off that confrontation as long as possible. It might be the coward's way, but she had Brand and maybe even their baby to consider now.

Brand ground his teeth and smiled. His wife was dancing with the deputy. All he wanted to do was cut in, but each of his new neighbors seemed to have a story to tell, including the man who now had him cornered by the punch bowl.

"Toni spent every summer and every Christmas holiday with Will for as far back as I kin remember. T'was good for her to get away from—" The man's wife elbowed him. He cleared his throat.

Brand frowned. What did Toni need to get away from?

The man tugged at the collar of his dress shirt. "I'd say Toni ran circles round Will, with the help of that foreman of his. It was Rusty who taught Toni to ride and shoot like a reg'lar ranch hand. Said she needed to learn to stick up for herself if—'' Again the wife's elbow interrupted him. ''Can't say Will liked her being a tomboy, but he did love that girl.''

Brand's face ached from smiling, and his mind churned. What didn't the woman want him to know? The sound of Toni's laughter drew his gaze across the yard. Excusing himself, Brand decided to reclaim his wife. He turned off the stereo and grabbed a couple of glasses of champagne punch. Everyone halted midstep. He caught Toni's gaze and lifted a glass.

''I'd like to propose a toast to my beautiful bride, the only woman I know who could make me give up the rodeo.'' Brand heard the exclamations of surprise, but what interested him most was the dismay on Toni's face.

Caleb yelled out, ''Why you wanna do a dang-fool thing like that when you could go for another world championship?''

Brand strolled across the yard, not once breaking eye contact with Toni. He pressed a plastic champagne flute into her hand and captured the other, tugging her away from Keegan. She watched him warily, and Brand couldn't blame her. He had a sudden urge to kiss his bride and not turn her loose until she lay exhausted in his arms. *Like she'd been in Vegas.*

Brand tried for a besotted expression. ''Toni and I want to start a family real soon. Can't do that if I'm never home.''

Objections bubbled in her eyes. Brand planted a swift kiss on her lips to keep her from voicing them. ''I always figured I'd quit once I found the right place to settle down.''

''And the right woman,'' added Cort.

Brand lifted his glass in agreement rather than correct his mistake. Cort would be disillusioned soon enough.

A rickety van pulled to a halt in the drive. The doors opened and cowboys spilled out. Brand grinned and nodded toward the van. ''Crew's here.''

"What crew?" Toni caught his sleeve.

"I hired some of my buddies to help out."

"Brand, we didn't discuss this." The sparks shooting from her eyes were hard to miss.

"We agreed on the basic stuff. These guys'll get it done."

"The basics—" Her nostrils flared as she took a deep breath. "I should have been in on the interviews."

Her breasts rose and fell rapidly. It was distracting as hell and made him feel like a hormone-driven adolescent again.

"There were no interviews, darlin'. I've known these guys for years. I gave 'em a call and here they are." What was the fuss about? Any crew was better than the one she'd had.

"And where do you think they'll sleep?"

"The bunkhouse."

The triumphant look in her eyes made him uneasy. Had it been a trick question? "I guess you haven't been inside the bunkhouse since the last crew left. They trashed the place, Brand. It'll take weeks to get it repaired."

Brand said a word that made her flinch. "Why didn't you say something, or call your buddy, the deputy, and report 'em for vandalism?"

"I did tell Josh, but we can't prove Matthews did it. I only discovered it yesterday. Neither of us went into the bunkhouse before the crew left."

Brand slammed his hand into his fist. Toni shrank away. It wasn't the first time the fear in her eyes contradicted her gutsy behavior. What was she afraid of? "Toni—"

"Trouble in paradise already?" Caleb's bitter tone asked for trouble.

"Take a hike, Caleb."

Toni stepped between them. "No, it's all right. Brand didn't realize we'd have to let his new crew share our house until the bunkhouse is repaired. I'm...upset at having a honeymoon for six." She wore a conciliatory smile, but her grip on Brand's hand could very likely break his bones.

Caleb grinned and Toni's grip loosened. "Not so bright, little brother. Can't they bunk in the barn or camp outside?"

Toni shook her head. "The weatherman is calling for rain, the tack room is overrun by rats, and the loft is full of hay. We have houseguests. Excuse me."

Toni looked from the elaborate three-tiered wedding cake one of her neighbors had labored over to the table laden with gifts. Unless she wanted to tell the guests that her marriage was a sham, she and Brand would be sharing a room. She scanned the happy faces and shook her head. These people had stood by her during some really rough times. She wouldn't disappoint them.

She felt queasy just contemplating sharing Brand's bed again. Their relationship was a temporary necessity, a means to an end. She wouldn't let it become more. She'd seen firsthand that love was a trap loaded with mental and physical pain.

Toni slipped into the house to move her things into Brand's room. She pulled out an armful of hangers. The ranch was her family's heritage. *She* was going to get it back into prime working order and keep right on running it once the wanderlust hit Brand again. Despite his unexpected announcement today, she didn't believe he'd give up the rodeo.

"Need some help?"

Toni yelped and spun around, scattering clothes in the process. Brand leaned against the doorjamb of her bedroom. He removed his suit coat and tossed it on the bed, then unfastened several buttons of his shirt. The exposed sliver of chest made Toni's hands tingle from the memory of firm flesh beneath her fingertips and the tickle of dark curls against her palms. He came toward her, jolting her heart into a dangerously fast pace with his slow, measured steps. Toni gathered her clothes and held them like a barrier between them.

"I'm moving my things to your room, but I can manage." In the intimacy of the bedroom she was afraid to lift her gaze higher than the middle of his chest. The room felt crowded and airless. This ridiculous hormonal reaction was exactly why she'd avoided Brand as much as possible over the past few days. When he entered a room, she left it. Now he blocked her path.

"I don't doubt it, darlin'. You seem capable of just about anything, but I'll help." Brand wrestled the clothes from her, his knuckles brushing her breasts in the process. He turned and disappeared into the hallway as if he hadn't heard her gasp.

Toni closed her eyes, inhaling and exhaling slowly. She tried to ignore the tingle of her nipples. She couldn't let him get to her. Grabbing more clothes, Toni headed for the master bedroom. Brand hung her things in the closet beside his own. Toni took one look at the wide bed, dumped her burden on it and bolted back to her room.

With her eyes closed she leaned back against the dresser, and tried to gather her shattered composure. This wasn't going to work. She couldn't pretend indifference when every hormone in her body had been on red alert since she'd spotted one dark-haired cowboy in that arena in Vegas. She'd broken her cardinal rule when she'd had sex with Brand, and he was tempting her to break it again. But she wouldn't. She'd vowed long ago not to get tangled up with another controlling, *physical* man. Her father had been enough to last a lifetime.

"Toni?"

She jerked her eyes open, surprised by his nearness when she hadn't heard him approach. Brand stood scant inches from her, his brow wrinkled in concern, his dark gaze intent on hers. Toni plastered herself against the dresser, gripping the edge until her knuckles ached. "Wh-what?"

She saw something in his eyes that looked like regret. "I won't lie to you and say I don't want you back in my bed, but I don't intend to force you." Toni flinched when he lifted his hand, but he only stroked a stray wisp of hair from her cheek. He noticed her involuntary gesture. She could see the questions in his eyes and cursed herself for revealing her fear. The delicate scrape of his fingertip had all her nerve endings clicking their heels in attention.

"We were good together, Toni." His husky words and those darned chocolate eyes sent her heart racing.

"I won't sleep with you." Who was she trying to convince with that quivery statement? Him? Or herself? It didn't matter. Neither one of them was listening. She frowned and pushed at his wrist. He resisted. Toni felt the strong, rapid beat of his pulse drumming beneath her fingers. It beat nearly as fast as her own. "I mean...I will *sleep* with you, but I won't...I...oh, hell."

Brand's other hand joined the first in cupping her face. With his thumbs, he tilted her chin until her eyes met his.

He stroked his thumb over her bottom lip and Toni's knees threatened to go on strike. "Making love is a lot like bull riding. It's as much a mental thing as it is a physical thing. Unless you're with me, it's not going to be any good." His gaze followed the path of his thumb, then returned to hers even hotter than before. "You were with me in Vegas, darlin', and it was damn near earth-shattering."

His head lowered, pausing with his mouth a scant inch away from hers. His breath fanned her lips. "Are you with me, Toni?"

She was. Despite all reason and fear. Beneath the heat of his gaze and the touch of his hands, she couldn't think, couldn't breathe. His deep voice mesmerized, beckoning her back to the ecstasy of that night. Toni's lips parted. She flushed hot then cold and wanted out of her clothes. She tightened her grip on his wrist. "Ye—"

Roy, the beefy calf roper, stood in the open door. "Hey, Brand, where you want us to stow our gear?"

Muttering an earthy curse, Brand dropped his hands and stepped away. Toni closed her eyes and silently thanked the blundering cowboy for interrupting what would have been a colossal mistake. What was wrong with her? Had she lost her mind?

"Starting the honeymoon already?" Roy leered and winked at Toni. The scowl on Brand's face had Roy throwing up his hands and backing out of the room. "Sorry."

"We'll finish this later," Brand promised before leading Roy down the hall to the spare bedroom.

Toni collapsed against the dresser. She was in trouble. Big, big trouble. She absolutely could not fall for Brand's potent charm again. In Vegas he'd worked his sorcery on her and made her forget all about finding an easygoing, irresponsible cowboy. Look how badly that had turned out. She now had a husband she didn't want and an entire town to witness her falling on her face.

Brand lay on the bed, his arms behind his head, striving to appear relaxed when he was anything but. The last of the wedding guests had vanished, leaving him with an overload of anticipation humming through his veins. Toni was in the bathroom. She'd turned the water off a good fifteen minutes ago, but he hadn't heard a sound from beyond the door since. He had a hunch she wasn't preparing for their wedding night, but he could hope. As a matter of fact, he'd bet his Finals check she was avoiding him. It wasn't a flattering thought for a guy who'd always had women chasing after him. Not that he'd taken advantage of the buckle bunnies, safety being an issue and all. That was probably why Toni had his hormones in an uproar. He'd been without a steady woman too long.

He checked the clock again. Why would she hide out in the bathroom? Their lovemaking in Vegas had damn near stopped his heart. He couldn't see any possible reason to avoid repeating something that incredible. He'd been gentle with her, even taken extra care to make sure her first time was a good experience.

Hell, it had been a fabulous experience. For both of them.

Hadn't it? Brand's gut twisted with doubt. Had Toni been faking it? Hell, no. She'd been wet and breathless. Her heart had pounded just as hard as his. He'd felt it beneath his hands and lips. Brand grew more tense as the minutes ticked by until he began thinking she might be sick or something.

Toni admitted she was stalling. She sat on the vanity counter and lectured her reflection. "Do not go out there and make a fool of yourself by crawling all over the man. It doesn't matter that he gave you the kind of wedding day dreams are made of—other people's dreams, that is. He's a heap of trouble in a Resistol. You are not going to get involved with him under any circumstances."

Her gaze dropped to her stomach, which she covered protectively with her hand. She was already in over her head, but she couldn't afford to let him get any closer. He'd leave, or he'd take over. Her child. Her ranch. Her life. She'd sworn she'd never give another man the power to hurt her.

Toni shivered. She'd been able to run to Grandpa Will before, but she couldn't run anymore, because she had no one and no place to run to. This time, she had to handle the situation on her own. Not only was her life at stake, so was her child's—if there was one.

Focus on the mission. Where had she gone wrong? Conceiving should have been as emotionally detached as visiting a sperm bank, only with a guarantee that the male contribution came from a real cowboy, not just some guy who lied and said he was one. But it hadn't been clinical. Brand Lander had reduced her to pleading and begging in a way she'd never anticipated. He'd made her weak and weakness was something she couldn't afford.

He'd been right, damn his sorry hide. She'd been with him. Every breath. Every whisper. Every touch. The memories of how gentle he'd been could still make her pulse flutter and her belly tighten. It wouldn't do. It just wouldn't do. Toni squared her shoulders and glared at her flushed face in the mirror. She had a plan. All she had to do was execute it.

"Don't look at him. Don't touch him. Just sleep. Piece of cake. You sleep every night of your life. Tonight's no different." Pulling in a deep breath, she reached for the door.

"Toni?" Brand rapped on the door.

She nearly jumped out of her skin. "Uh… Yeah?"

"What in the hell are you doing in there?"

Toni yanked open the door, intent on telling him to get off her case. The words dried up. Brand wore nothing but underwear. Very *brief* briefs, which left little to the imagination. His hair stood in spikes, as if he'd been raking his fingers through it. A lone curl, the one she'd twined around her finger in Vegas, flopped across his forehead. Her hormones rioted.

"You all right?" He rubbed a hand across his bare chest. Toni's fingers tingled as if she could actually feel the wiry curls herself. The man had a magnificent chest.

Dragging her gaze from his pectorals, she focused on the crooked lampshade beyond his shoulder and reminded her lungs that they had a job to do, because they weren't doing it well. She felt light-headed. "F-fine. I'm fine. Just sleepy. Very sleepy. Good night."

She sidled around him and headed toward the bed with the determination of a salmon swimming upstream. *Oh, bad analogy. Salmon went upstream to reproduce.* She didn't even want to think about that right now.

"Whose shirt is that?" Brand's hand on her shoulder stopped her. It sent a flash of heat clear down to her womb.

For precious moments, Toni fought the urge to turn in his arms and put his hands on her aching breasts.

Go to sleep before you get yourself in trouble, you idiot. She inhaled slowly and turned to face him, but she kept her eyes focused on his. She would not look at his broad chest or the flat nipples she knew were as sensitive as her own. She would not notice the way the dark triangle of hair narrowed until it became a thin line leading from the navel she'd tickled with her tongue to his—

Toni jerked her head back up and cursed herself for doing exactly what she'd promised herself she wouldn't. Her heart beat so hard she was sure he could hear it. "M-my grandfather's. I d-didn't have anything else to s-sleep in."

Brand's jaw dropped. Closing his mouth and eyes, he dropped his head back and groaned. The hand on her shoulder tightened—not enough to hurt—then dropped away. "You sleep in the raw?"

Toni felt a blush climbing from her toes clear up to her ears. She may have renounced the prissy ways her parents had tried to force on her, but she hadn't been able to dismiss her love for silky underthings. She didn't own a single piece of lingerie that was anything less than an invitation to any man who saw it. She certainly wasn't wearing that kind of thing to bed with Brand because he wasn't the type to ignore the invitation. Despite the lecture she'd given herself, she wasn't sure she could resist if he pushed. Toni rubbed her temple. As a matter of fact, she was pretty sure she'd cave then hate herself in the morning. "I'll be comfortable in this."

"That's not what I asked," he said, tugging her chin around until their eyes met. "What do you usually sleep in?"

Toni couldn't think with his hand sliding down her arm to capture and stroke her fingers. He did it with such gentleness. His eyes glistened. *Get in that bed and go to sleep, Antonia Swenson. Lander.* She lifted her lids, which seemed determined to close, not because she was sleepy, but because her blood had heated to a thick ooze. Yanking her hand away, she opened a drawer, grabbed the nightie on top and flung it in his face. "I usually sleep in this."

While he gaped, she dived into bed, yanked the covers up to her chin, and hugged her edge of the mattress.

Brand caught the scrap of lace as it struck his face. Seeing Toni in another man's shirt had irked him. The shirttail flapping against her bare thighs had his groin throbbing with the memory of Toni wearing his shirt in Vegas. They'd awoken hungry and ordered a middle-of-the-night buffet. Afterward, she'd wrapped those shapely thighs of hers around his waist while he slowly unbuttoned… Oh, man.

The silky pink material slipping through his fingers only exacerbated his desire. Darned if he wouldn't have been better off thinking she slept naked rather than picturing her in this peek-a-boo piece of sin.

He was hard and hurting. And it looked as though he'd stay like that if the way Toni clung to her edge of the bed was anything to go by. She sent out more cold than a chunk of dry ice. He tossed the gown back into the drawer.

"Dammit, Toni. This is ridiculous." Easing her legs out of the way, he sat beside her.

She scowled. "I did not want a husband. You're the one who insisted we marry." Rolling over, she presented him with her back.

Brand stroked a knuckle down her stiff spine. Even though she stiffened up, he didn't miss her shiver or the hitch in her breathing. "There's nothing to say we can't make the best of the situation."

She glared at him over her shoulder.

Brand sighed and stood. He wasn't going to beg. He adjusted his briefs and circled the bed to crawl beneath the covers. Rolling to his side to face her, he propped his head on his elbow. Their eyes met for one brief moment. He dragged a fingertip along her arm. For some reason he couldn't help touching her petal-soft skin. "Toni, there's so much more I could teach you about making love."

"It wasn't making love, Brand. It was sex. Procreation. Pure and simple." She squeezed her eyes shut.

Brand snorted and lay on his back, folding his hands beneath his head. "Darlin', there was nothing pure or simple about that night in Vegas. We were about as sinful and tangled up as a man and woman can get."

She yanked the covers up to her ears. From the flush on her skin and her unsteady breathing, Brand knew he could probably change her mind with a little effort, but he wanted her willing.

Toni tried holding her breath, but it didn't work. She might not have to look at him, talk to him or even touch him, but she could *smell* him. For crying out loud. He'd showered before her. It was bad enough that his scent had hung in the bathroom when her turn had come, invading her space when he wasn't in sight. Now, in the cover of darkness, with nothing more than a shaft of moonlight crossing the bed, his woodsy scent again invaded her space, her mind. It made her ache. She pulled the sheet over her nose and chased sleep.

Her resistance weakened. It *had* been good in Vegas. Brand had been an ardent lover. She hadn't known that a man could make magic with his hands, his mouth, his body. She hadn't known that the rough groan of a man's voice, urging her to climb the peak one more time, could be so sexy. She hadn't known that lovemaking could be fast and urgent, slow and tender, or any number of variations in between.

She'd never known a man could be so gentle.

After her father's last tirade, the counselors had assured her that not all men were violent, but she hadn't believed them. Could they be right? Brand hadn't raised his hand in anger. *Yet,* her mind cautioned. She eased onto her side. For precious moments she let her hand hover over Brand's chest, anticipating the feel of him, the taste of him, the weight of him.

Down the hall the bathroom door squeaked open as one of the ranch hands got up. Toni jerked her hand back. Brand was a man. Of course she couldn't trust him.

Six

Déjà vu. A muscle-corded arm pinned Toni to the bed and a tanned hand cupped her breast. Brand's hard thigh fit intimately between hers, and his body heat seared her from her ankles to the back of her neck. His breath teased her hair, causing goose bumps to chase across her skin and her nipple to peak beneath his palm.

Toni gritted her teeth against the bud of desire unfurling in her belly and eased onto her back. First job of the day: extricating herself from the bed without waking her husband.

Her husband. She lay back and swallowed. Brand muttered something in his sleep and contracted his fingers. Toni gasped as lightning shot from her breast to her womb. Even in his sleep he knew what to do with a woman!

Brand jerked awake. He blinked once, twice. A slow, sleepy smile curved his lips. His eyes went from foggy to fiery in a nanosecond, and Toni's heart rate doubled just as fast.

"Mornin'," he said in a voice as raspy as his face. His thumbnail scratched over her nipple, finding it easily through her grandfather's chambray shirt. The place between her thighs tingled. *Danger* flashed in her mind like a street sign.

"Let me up, Brand." Was that her voice? That husky plea? Dear heavens. Toni put her hand on his thigh, determined to shove him off her and bolt for the bathroom. She hadn't counted on his hot skin scorching her palm or his wiry hairs tickling her nerve endings until she forgot all about running. Forgot everything but the feel of his skin next to hers.

Brand's arms banded around her and with an easy flip, he had her tucked beneath him. The heat of him scorched her through the tangled sheets. His mouth hovered, then brushed lightly against hers. Toni struggled with her need for safety and an overwhelming hunger to touch him, to stroke the hot, satiny skin of his back, to feel him inside her.

Rap. Rap. Wade, the youngest of the new crew, stood in the open bedroom door staring at the ceiling. His face and neck were nearly as red as his hair. "Uh…boss, you gonna get up? We're waiting for orders. It's nearly eight, and you said we needed to get going ASAP," he said, his tone apologetic.

Embarrassed beyond belief, Toni tried to hide beneath Brand.

"Be right down," Brand told him. Once the footsteps faded Brand closed his eyes and flopped back onto his side of the bed with a groan. "I know I shut that door last night," he growled irritably, then threw the covers back.

Toni started counting the stripes on the sheet to keep herself from watching Brand dress. Squeezing her eyes shut, she acknowledged it wasn't fear making her heart race. She cleared her throat and picked at the pillowcase. "The lock won't catch, so the door won't stay shut."

"I'll fix it. But first, I'm gonna warn those yahoos about

interrupting us. I swear I'll castrate the next one." He sounded angry enough to carry out the threat. Toni's eyes flew open. Brand had on his jeans and was stuffing his arms into another one of his flashy shirts. This one was white with a vivid herd of horses galloping across the sunset depicted on his back.

"Brand, don't you have any...work clothes?" She bit her lip and tried not to wince when he turned and she saw the front was twice as bright as the back. But at least she'd distracted him from his anger. She was very good at defusing anger. She'd had to be from an early age.

He glanced at his shirt and shrugged. "These *are* my work clothes. My sponsors give me the clothes, boots and hats, and pay me to wear them. If I'm dressed, darlin', I'm working. You'll get used to 'em eventually. I did." He grinned and Toni's breath hitched. "Best I remember, it took a while though."

He stepped into the bathroom. When he came out he put on his hat and turned for the door. "I'm going to get the boys started on the bunkhouse."

He left and Toni threw his pillow at the door. Darn it, she didn't want the bunkhouse fixed. Twice now, one of the men had kept her from doing something stupid.

Shoving aside the covers, she crossed the room and shut the bedroom door. She used one of the boxes of Brand's belongings his family had left behind yesterday to block it closed. She'd just tugged off her nightshirt and panties when the bedroom door opened. Toni squealed and tried to cover herself with her hands.

"What the he—" Brand looked up from the box he'd kicked aside and his words stopped. His gaze narrowed, raking slowly over her with bone-melting thoroughness. Stepping inside, he removed his hat, closed the door, and kicked the makeshift doorstop back into place.

"The men are working outside." His voice was rough. Toni's skin heated beneath his scrutiny. She kept one arm over her breasts and the other over her lap. "Y-you should kn-knock."

"On my own door?" His nostrils flared. After another lingering perusal of her nudity, his gaze met hers.

Toni squeezed her eyes shut and turned away from the invitation in his eyes. She heard him move closer and every muscle in her tensed. "P-please leave."

"Look at me," Brand's voice commanded in her ear.

She could feel his closeness, his heat and his breath stirring her hair. Reluctantly, she obeyed. In the mirror, she saw him behind her completely clothed, while she was totally naked. Her insides tightened. Her breath shuddered. She felt vulnerable. And weak. And aroused. And powerful. How did he do that? How could he exude such strength and yet make her feel strong at the same time?

He lifted his hand, and Toni braced herself against the touch she saw coming but was unable to resist. Brand dragged a fingertip down her arm, setting off an explosion, like a string of firecrackers in its wake.

His beard-roughened kiss on the sensitive spot beneath her ear electrified her. His hands settled on her waist, pulling her against him. "Let's go back to bed."

The denim of his jeans felt rough as he pressed himself against her bottom, while the pearlized snaps of his shirt felt cool against her spine. Toni's eyelids grew heavy.

"We can't." She exhaled the words. Brand nipped her earlobe. Her resistance faded beneath the sensuous glide of his hands over her hips, back up to the outer curves of her breasts. The reasons why they shouldn't be doing this burst like balloons.

He slid his tongue down the tendons of her neck. "Let me love you, Ton—"

A door slammed downstairs. One of the crew bellowed, "Brand! Time's a wastin'. Let's head out."

Brand muttered a curse and tightened his hands on her waist. "I used to like that man." Compressing his lips, Brand put a few inches between them. "You're right.

Now's not the time. I'm heading for town to pick up supplies. Need anything?''

Toni could barely remember her name, let alone her shopping requirements. ''I have a list on my desk. We need to repair the wells and reseed the pastures before the weather changes.''

''Toni—'' A horn blew outside. Brand heaved a sigh and settled his hat on his head. ''I'll see you in a few hours.''

Then he was gone. Toni sank onto the chair, her body still quivering from his caress. *Idiot. You didn't last five seconds with him once he turned on the charm. All he had to do was breathe on you.*

Toni cleaned the debris from the bunkhouse and piled it in the side yard for burning. She mucked the stalls and fed all the horses. She'd just finished reloading the mousetraps when Brand returned. A delivery truck bearing the Farm and Ranch Supply logo followed his truck. She greeted the driver, whom she'd known for years, then walked alongside the flatbed, looking for seed, pump parts and barbed wire. All she saw was building materials. Next she searched the bed of Brand's truck. Groceries. Horse feed. No pump. No fencing. No seed. Her temper stirred. Hands on hips, she faced him. ''Brand, where's my stuff?''

Brand nudged his hat back and hooked his thumbs through his belt loops. ''We'll get it after we get the bunkhouse repaired.''

''We agreed. The wells and pastures are top priority,'' she pointed out. ''The cattle dip and inoculant are next.''

His jaw firmed. ''As of this morning, the bunkhouse became top priority.''

Toni felt her cheeks heat as the men listened attentively. ''Getting the crew out of the house will not change things,'' she whispered angrily.

''If you say so, darlin'.'' Brand's lips tilted up in a naughty grin. Hot sparks radiated from his eyes.

The urge to smack the know-it-all look off his handsome face stunned her. She'd *never* felt violent toward another person—not even her father. "Brand, we agreed to fix the wells and fences first."

"No, darlin', we didn't."

"I... You..." She was so angry she was sputtering. If she didn't get away from him, she *was* going to hit him, and hitting was never the answer. This was her ranch, she reminded herself. Brand was only a temporary investor here. Once he had his fill of solitude and hard work, he'd go back to the excitement of rodeoing and adoring buckle bunnies.

She turned on her heel and stomped into the house, determined to find the money somewhere to buy the pumps and fencing. An hour later, the bottom line still read broke, or at least near it. She wasted a moment wishing her grandfather had converted his records to computer, but at least he wrote legibly. Although he'd never gone beyond sixth grade, his letters were carefully printed in the proper school-taught style except for a few sloppy entries on the last few pages. Toni stuck her pencil behind her ear and frowned. Why hadn't she noticed that the last time she went through the ledger? Because she'd been crying then.

Toni bent over the pages and felt a surge of guilt. Had Granddad's illness caused the change in his handwriting? She should have been here to help out, but she'd been finishing school and training her replacement at the vet's office.

Half an hour later she sat back in dismay. The bank statement showed a large sum of money had already been withdrawn from the ranch account. The amount matched the estimate she'd found on well costs. Only there weren't any new well pumps or rolls of fencing. She and Brand had covered every inch of the property. She would have seen the items lying around if they'd been purchased, or she would have found the cash when she packed up her grandfather's clothes. Double-checking the dates and the handwriting, Toni noted that the sloppy entries came just days before her grandfather's death. Where was the money if the equipment hadn't been bought?

She called the bank and asked for the manager.

"Your grandfather's foreman made the withdrawal for him, Mrs. Lander. Your grandfather wasn't feeling well, and he couldn't make the trip to town. I checked with the Billings brothers before releasing the money. They verified that the parts had been ordered."

Toni sat up straighter in the chair. There was no work order from Billings Brothers' Well-Drilling Company. "Did the withdrawal slip have my grandfather's signature on it?"

"Are you suggesting he didn't authorize the withdrawal?" The man's voice chilled considerably.

"I'm saying, Mr. Richards, that the money was withdrawn for repairs, and the equipment to make them is not on the ranch. Neither is the cash. Mr. Matthews is not listed on the account."

He put her on hold. Toni impatiently thumped her pencil on the desk. She wouldn't put it past Matthews to rob a dying man.

"Miss Anderson, the signature doesn't seem to be…as neat as your grandfather's. I've also spoken with Lettie Billings. The well parts haven't been paid for or picked up."

"And if the signature is forged?" Hope flickered within her breast. It wasn't enough to bail out the ranch, but it would help her get the upper hand with one pigheaded cowboy.

"Then the bank will cover the funds, and we'll prosecute the forger. It's a federal offense to obtain money under false pretenses. We'll do our best to rectify the situation." Now the banker sounded overeager to please. Funny how her mistake had made him hoity. His mistake made him simper.

Toni ended the call and went in search of Brand. She

found him in the bunkhouse, stripped to the waist, a new tool belt hanging low on his hips. *Sexy.* The word popped into her brain before she could squash it. Muscles flexed and bunched beneath his sweat-slickened back as he pounded nails into a sheet of paneling on the wall.

"Brand?" Her voice was breathless and weak. She had to repeat herself to be heard over the hammering.

He lowered the hammer and faced her. "Yeah?"

Sweat tricked over his stubbly jaw, down his chest, and over his lean abdomen to dampen the waistband of his jeans. One droplet disappeared into his navel—the navel she'd dipped her tongue into. He cleared his throat, wiped his arm across his forehead and arched a dark brow.

Toni dropped her eyes to the paper crushed in her palm and pulled in a slow breath, willing the vision of rippling muscles to vacate her brain. Her blood raced and it had nothing to do with fear. "I…I think I've discovered where Matthews found the money for his new truck."

Brand slotted the hammer into his tool belt. "Show me."

Toni led him back to the house and into the study. She bent over the ledger, pointing wordlessly to the sloppy entries, because she couldn't find her voice. Brand leaned over the desk, his hands bracketing her body. The clean scent of fresh perspiration and the heat of his body filled her senses.

"What can we do about it?" Brand didn't draw back. He merely turned his head. His breath fanned her cheek.

Toni cleared her throat and focused on the scratches in the surface of the old desk rather than on the curve of Brand's lips. "The bank manager said the bank would have to make the money good if it's their mistake."

Brand nodded, his expression thoughtful as he straightened. He squeezed her shoulder. "Good job."

"As soon as it's cleared, I'm going to have the wells repaired and buy the seed." Taking one step back then another, she thrust out her chin and dared him to dispute it.

Brand sighed and scraped a hand across his face. "I'll get those, Toni. Put the money aside. You might…need it."

"Why?" She frowned.

"In case one of us doesn't hang around." Brand turned on his heel and left.

Toni scowled after him. A chill skipped down her spine. He had that right. One of them definitely wasn't the settling-down kind, but it wasn't her.

"What in the hell are you doing?"

The hammer slipped from Toni's fingers. She dug her nails into the roofing felt to keep from following the tool down the steep slope to the ground. "Stop creeping up on me."

Brand stood at the top of the ladder. "You have no business up here. Get down."

As hot as it was on the black tar paper, the temperature shot up another dozen degrees under his glare. "Wrong, cowboy. This ranch and anything on it is my business. Go bother somebody else."

"Get down." Brand knelt on the blacktop, as immovable as a gargoyle, but not nearly as ugly. Unfortunately. His sweat-soaked white T-shirt clung to his chest, as transparent as wet tissue. It was distracting, to say the least, to a woman who didn't want to topple to the ground below.

Golden sparks shot from his deep brown eyes and he'd thinned his luscious lips to an angry slash. And his jeans… She blew out a breath. With the way they clung and cupped him, her balance was in serious jeopardy. "Go away, Brand. I need to finish before the rain starts."

"Get down or I'll carry you down." The words were quietly, but adamantly spoken.

"What's the matter? Can't stand to have a woman above you?" Toni knew from the sudden glint in his eye, that she should have kept her smart mouth shut. What was wrong with her? Provoking someone was something she usually avoided at all costs, but it seemed she had a subconscious wish to push Brand until he snapped. At least then she'd know his limits.

"I have no problem with a woman over me or under me, darlin'. You should know. You've been both."

Heat flashed through her like a lit match. Toni told herself she had to get off the roof to get her hammer anyway. It had nothing to do with the sudden light-headedness she experienced when he turned on that bedroom voice and reminded her of Vegas.

Brand stayed one rung below her while she descended the ladder. She didn't know whether to be irritated that he coddled her or touched over his concern. Once she had both feet on the ground, she turned, intent on going to work in some Brand-less location. His hands still gripped the ladder on either side of her shoulders, trapping her between the metal rungs and hard, muscled cowboy. Reluctantly, she met his gaze.

"Let the guys do the dangerous stuff. It's what I'm paying 'em for." With a nod of his head, he was gone.

Brand figured the woman was going to give him a heart attack. Despite her pint size she seemed determined to take on jobs clearly better suited to a man. A part of him said let her break her dang-fool neck. The other part wanted her doing less hazardous chores. Hell, she didn't have to prove her worth to him. He'd already figured out there wasn't anything on this ranch she couldn't handle. There was something about a woman who looked as delicate as an angel but was as tough and determined as a veteran bull rider that set him on his heels.

In the meantime, between her escapades and the fact that she looked like every cowboy's dream in her tight jeans and tank tops, it didn't look like his heart was ever going to catch its normal rhythm again. He'd probably keel over before he saw this place running smoothly. It was a shame she wouldn't stick around. They could've been quite a team.

He was acting like a spoiled kid who wanted what he couldn't have, and he knew it, but Toni made him ache for something he couldn't put a tag on. Part of it was the memory of that night in Vegas, but part of it was... something else.

He found himself looking forward to their shared cup of coffee each morning and again after dinner. He liked the easy way she teased the men, keeping 'em in line with an arch of her brow or a fist on her hip. She might be a little slip of a thing, but the men all liked and respected her. Problem was, he was beginning to, too. She was smart and funny. If they'd met under different circumstances... Nah, he didn't believe in marriage because he'd seen it fail too many times. If he hadn't *had* to marry her, he wouldn't have.

He stepped into the shade of the bunkhouse porch, mentally counting the days since Vegas. When would she know if she was pregnant? Would she tell him or would he have to pry it out of her? His stomach did a funny twist. The possibility of being a father to a tiny helpless baby scared him spitless, but it also left him with a determination to do right by his kid. He'd seen enough happy families on the circuit to know a kid needed more than three square meals a day. A kid needed to know he was loved— doubly so if one of the parents had taken off. A kid needed to know he was more than just free labor and an obligation.

And a kid needed hugs. He couldn't remember the last time somebody had hugged him. *His* kid would have hugs.

The screen door slammed. Brand nearly dropped the new door he and Roy were hanging on the bunkhouse when Toni came off the back porch wearing a dress. He'd forgotten she had a first-class pair of legs, a tiny waist and a great set of— "Yeeeeow, damn it all to hell, Roy. You dropped the door on my foot."

"Sorry, Brand." Roy flushed and lifted his side of the door. His appreciative gaze shifted back to Toni. "Ya sure married you a looker."

The wind caught Toni's skirt, ballooning it up and out and giving him a peek at her sleek thighs. The view sent a flash of heat to his groin. That woman's legs were meant to be worn like a belt—around his waist. Shame was, she didn't agree.

Brand heard more than one wolf whistle and glared at his crew. "Put your eyes back in your heads. Roy, hold that door level. Wade, take over for me here." Brand passed the drill to the blushing kid and jogged over to meet Toni at the car.

"Where you headed?" She looked fabulous, and he wanted to drag her straight to bed. She'd put on her pink lipstick. The familiar urge to smear it with his mouth hit him just before the flowery scent of her perfume nearly knocked him to his knees.

Toni stepped around him and headed to the car. "I'm going to the bank to get the money straightened out."

"I'll come with you."

She frowned and glanced at her watch. "I have a nine o'clock appointment. I don't have time to wait for you to get ready."

Brand glanced at his clothes. He had on one of his sponsor-provided shirts. It had red lightning bolts on a black background. The colors were a little loud, but both the shirt and his black jeans were clean. "There's something wrong with what I'm wearing?"

Toni's gaze swept slowly over him. His blood headed south under her slow perusal. If the wave of pink flush creeping up her neck was any indication, she'd noticed his response.

"Let's go." She slid into the driver's seat of her aged sedan and fired the engine.

Brand knew without a doubt if he didn't drop his tool belt pronto and get in, she'd leave him behind. One thing he'd learned about Toni was that she didn't waste time when something needed doing. He tossed the belt to Aaron and settled in the seat.

Inside the bank, employees stepped forward to congratulate them on their marriage. One woman dragged Toni off to her desk to see a picture of her latest grandchild. Brand felt a frisson slither down his spine. Toni had roots here. Would she leave as soon as he expected? Sure, she would.

Toni beckoned him from an open office door. "Mr. Richards is ready for us."

Richards was a typical banker. High-dollar suit, wire-rimmed glasses and slicked-back hair. Brand would bet the man had never sipped from a longneck bottle in his life. After shaking Brand's hand with his soft palm, he gestured to the chairs opposite his desk, and closed the door before launching into a suck-up monologue.

Brand interrupted. "Let's cut to the chase. We want the money back in the ranch account with all due interest. Toni and I'll need our names on the signature card and new checks printed." Brand sat back in his chair. "If you can handle that, I'll transfer my personal accounts to your bank."

As expected, the man squirmed like an overeager puppy. "I'll get the forms immediately." He hustled out of the office.

Toni rolled her eyes. "I haven't seen that much brown-nosing on a new calf searching his momma for his first meal."

"Don't take it personally. It's my money he wants."

Richards bustled in, fanned out several signature cards and an assortment of forms across his desk. He pointed to the first two. "These are the signature cards for the Rocking A accounts. If you'll both sign those where marked?" He shifted several other cards. "These will be for your new accounts…unless, of course, you'd like to deposit all of your funds into the ranch account?''

"Nope." Brand shook his head. "Keeping it separate."

Richards nodded. "So all we'll need to do is transfer your funds to this bank and add Toni—" he flashed Toni a fond smile "—Mrs. Lander's signature to your signature card."

"This'll be my personal account." There was no way in hell he'd give the woman a chance to clean out his money.

After a moment of uncomfortable silence the banker said, "Of course, Mr. Lander. Many young couples keep separate accounts these days. I should have asked instead of assuming."

Despite the quick recovery of the banker, Brand knew from the starch in Toni's spine that she wasn't happy. After concluding their business, Brand followed her from the bank. She climbed into her car without waiting for him to open her door. Brand had to hustle around the trunk and jump in as she shifted into reverse.

Toni reached the end of the city limits and hit the gas pedal. The deputy merely waved when the blue sedan blew past him at the speed of light. If there was a decent bone in the man's body, he'd have pulled her over. A few miles down the road, she swung the car into the Farm and Ranch Supply parking lot.

"Toni, my rodeoing is a separate business," he said, unclenching his fingers. "For tax purposes—"

She threw open her car door, slammed it in his face, and marched for the steps. Why in the hell did he feel so bad for doing the right thing? Brand swore and hustled to catch up. He grabbed her arm and spun her around. She jerked back as if she expected him to hit her, which angered and confused him even more. How could she think he'd hurt her, or any woman for that matter?

"You'll get the money you need for the ranch. Hell, I'm

going to deposit your half of the property value in the account as soon as the appraiser's report comes back."

Fire shot from her baby blues. How he'd ever thought she looked angelic, he didn't know. She looked positively lethal.

She pushed his hand away. "What I wanted was not to be totally humiliated by my husband. You might as well have taken out a front-page article in the weekly paper announcing that you didn't trust me with *your* money. It's the only bank in town, Brand. The one place everyone has in common. It's also the biggest source of gossip."

He thought he saw tears sparkling in her eyes, but she turned from him and threw open the glass door to the store. Everyone inside looked elsewhere. Brand swore again. Two stops in town. Two strikes against him.

Toni stepped to the counter and greeted the clerk by name. After a few minutes of chitchat she handed the man her list. "Brand forgot to pick up these the other day. Would you please have them delivered to the ranch tomorrow?"

She pulled out her checkbook and started writing. Brand stepped forward to remind her that he was supposed to be paying, but he held back. Making an issue of the money in front of the store personnel and customers was not the way to handle it. He'd deposit the amount of the check in the farm account next time he came to town.

"Mr. Lander?" the clerk called. "That fencing you ordered will be in tomorrow. Do you want us to deliver it with Toni's supplies?"

Toni frowned. "What fencing material? You said you didn't get anything on my list."

"The bull pen."

"We do our breeding by insemination."

Brand ran a finger under his collar. He'd meant to discuss his plans with her, but…well, with the way his hormones had been in an uproar, he'd forgotten. He glanced at the eavesdropping clerk and customers, then back to

Toni. "I'm building a corral and chutes for bucking bulls. I've bought a couple, and they'll be delivered within the week."

Color ran up her cheeks. It didn't stop until it reached her hairline. Her mouth opened and closed, then she pressed her lips together. Toni positively vibrated with anger. He wouldn't have been surprised if she'd taken a swing at him. "The Rocking A is a beef-cattle operation."

"I know, and we'll get back to that, eventually, but right now I want to give lessons to the kids coming along, Toni. Might even try to raise a few head of Brahma for the circuit."

Toni stared at him. Without another word, she walked out. Brand hustled behind her and hopped into the car. He had a feeling she'd like to leave him behind. A few miles down the road, she swerved to the shoulder.

Toni turned to him with a jerk. "Thank you for your repeated displays of confidence. First—" the gesture displaying a single finger was not a polite one "—you hire hands without consulting me. Second, you ignore my supply list in some mistaken belief that getting your buddies out of the house will have you sharing more than just my mattress. Third, your humiliating lack of confidence in me at the bank, and now this." She smacked the steering wheel. "Fifty-fifty, you said. When do I get a say in how *my family's ranch* is run?" Her voice had risen several decibels.

"Toni—"

"Get out," she said quietly. Her hands tightened on the steering wheel until her knuckles turned white. He figured she'd probably rather wrap 'em around his neck.

"What?" Brand shoved back his hat and laughed, thinking she was joking, but her glare could have set a dry field ablaze.

"Get out."

Brand got out.

Toni drove down the road a couple of miles and pulled

over. She shook so badly she could barely put the car in Park. If she hadn't made Brand get out of the car she would have hit him. *Hit him.* Never in her life had she met anyone who could arouse her to this degree of anger. *You are not your father,* the counselors had told her. She had to wonder. Today, she'd almost decked a cowboy.

She hadn't known Brand was considering raising bulls or teaching bull riding, because he hadn't bothered to tell her. High-handed. That's what he was. Devious and conniving. At least about the ranch. He was pretty darn honest about wanting more sex. With the crew he was kind, compassionate, loyal and generous. But with her....

She'd had enough negativity from her father, who'd been a firm believer in keeping the women in his life in the dark and under his thumb. According to him, a woman's role was to look good and support her husband's career. Her grandfather had offered her a safe refuge, but he'd also believed a woman's job was to support her man. Well she didn't want to support a man. She wanted to support herself.

If it hadn't been for her grandfather's former foreman, she wouldn't have been allowed out of the ranch compound. Rusty had sneaked her out on the trail. He'd taught her how to ride, rope, shoot, brand and just about everything else that needed doing on the ranch. He'd never held her back because she was female. He'd treated her like one of the hands. In the process he'd gifted her with a confidence in herself and her abilities, something she'd sorely lacked.

All she'd ever wanted was to come home to the Rocking A. If Brand thought he was going to take over, then she'd straighten him out pretty darn quick. And if she couldn't do it by herself, she'd find old Rusty. What that man could do with an unruly cowboy was legendary.

Seven

Brand kicked a rock and added another yard to the blue streak he'd been swearing along the roadside. Women were a pain. He'd be damned if he knew why men put up with them.

A memory of Vegas steamed his brain cells and ignited his groin. All right, he knew why. He'd put up with a lot to get Toni back in his bed. Or to see her face over his coffee mug each morning. He could talk to her. Didn't matter whether it was feed rations or baseball. She didn't fuss about clothes, breaking a fingernail, or getting dirty like other women. And her ideas for the ranch blew his mind.

As if his day hadn't started out bad enough, the deputy sheriff's car pulled to a stop beside him. "Need a ride?"

The ranch was a good ten miles down the road. Except for that one night, he'd never been stupid. Brand swallowed his pride, opened the cruiser door, and climbed in. "'Preciate it."

They rode in silence for several minutes. Josh cleared his throat. "I know you don't want to hear this from me, but Toni has a hard time with men who try to boss her around. She had more than her share of that from her dad, and Will near 'bout smothered her. From what I've heard, either you didn't know or you don't care."

Brand digested the information. It explained a lot about some of the things that set Toni off. He turned in the seat, propped his elbow on the door, and eyed Keegan suspiciously. "You playing marriage counselor?"

Josh grimaced. "Nah. I just want Toni to be happy. If you're the one who makes her happy, then..." He shrugged.

Brand narrowed his eyes. "And if I don't?"

Keegan turned into the ranch driveway. Once he'd parked the cruiser behind the house, he turned off the ignition and faced Brand. "Then somebody else will."

Brand felt his territorial hackles rise. "Thanks for the warning, but Toni is *my* wife."

Again Josh shrugged. "If you can keep her. See, folks around here know things about Toni that you don't."

"And I know things about her that *you* don't. Thanks for the ride, Deputy, but stay away from Toni."

The aromas coming from the kitchen made Brand's mouth water and his stomach growl. He hung up his hat as Toni set lasagna, salad and crusty bread on the table. The hands were grumbling good-naturedly, but loading their plates with everything, including the veggies Toni insisted they eat.

She did more than her share of the kitchen duties and for that he gave thanks. He and the men knew how to cook steak and hamburger, hamburger and steak. All of it medium rare. And none of it with anything green near it except maybe a pickle.

"Hey, darlin'." She sidestepped his kiss. Brand shook his head and picked up a plate. Obviously she wasn't interested in making amends.

Toni seated herself at the far end of the table from him and addressed the ranch hands. "Can any of you drive the John Deere? I'd like to get started on the seeding while the weather's cooperating, and if a couple of you could help me with the fencing I'd appreciate it."

Deke frowned at Brand. "I thought the bull pen was next."

"Right after the bunkhouse, you said," Aaron insisted.

Wade watched wide-eyed, as if expecting an explosion. Roy smirked.

Brand looked at Toni's stiff shoulders and tight features. "Toni, the bulls have already left Cheyenne. I need Deke and Aaron to help me build the pens and Wade and Roy to help with set-up."

"Fine." She stood, scraped the food she hadn't touched into the trash, then headed for the office and quietly shut the door.

Four sets of eyes studied him as if he'd just drop-kicked a puppy. Brand growled, "Eat your damn dinners."

Toni sank into the leather chair, and put her head in her hands. Brand didn't trust her. She didn't even think he liked her. How could they have a marriage, even a temporary one, without those basics to build on? And if there was a baby, how could she bring it up in such a combative atmosphere?

The ranch wasn't her refuge anymore. It was a war zone with each of them trying to score hits off the other. So far, the hits had been verbal, but what would it take to push Brand over the line?

She reached for the phone to do the chore she'd been avoiding. "Mom—"

"Toni, good heavens child, where are you?" Without pausing for an answer she swept on, "We've been expecting you to come home as soon as you closed up Daddy's place. Your father has already contacted a Realtor about selling the ranch."

Toni counted to ten. "Mom, I'm staying here at the ranch."

"But Antonia, you can't handle that place alone, and I—I'd like to have you near."

Toni felt a stab of guilt. Maybe she should have stayed and stood up for her mother instead of running away, but the counselors had assured her that she had to get out while she could, before her father's brainwashing convinced her that she deserved the abuse. Still, leaving her mother behind had been difficult. She'd always regret it.

"Mom, I called to tell you that I got married last week."

"Without your father meeting him first and making sure he was an acceptable husband? What were you thinking?"

She bit her tongue on the retort that sprang to her lips and sighed. Fighting with her mother wasn't why she'd called. "His name is Brand Lander. You may have seen his picture in the paper. He's the National Finals Rodeo bull-riding champion this year."

"You married a man who rides bulls for a living!"

Why did talking to her mother always give her a headache? "Look, Mom, I've got to go…tend to a horse. Talk to you later."

Toni hung up on her mother's sputtering and pressed her fingers against her temples. That hadn't gone well. Not that she'd expected it would. She could only hope that her call to Rusty Jackson, her grandfather's previous foreman, would go better. She reached for her grandfather's Rolodex and crossed her fingers.

Perspiration rolled down Brand's face, but his skin felt clammy. His heart hammered triple-time. Inching backward, he never took his eyes from the snake coiled beside the wall on the far side of the stall. He heard someone enter the barn.

"Brand?"

He'd expected a confrontation, but he couldn't handle

it *now*. He had to warn her, but it was difficult to get anything past the terror clogging his throat. "Get out."

"What?"

"Snake. Get the hell out." He tried to talk without moving his lips.

He felt her presence directly behind him. "What kind?"

"A live one, dammit. Now move." She leaned past him. Crowding him. *Blocking his escape.* Every cell in his being tensed. Brand slowly spread his arms and tried to shield her. He eased backward. One step. Two.

Toni clasped his waist and planted her feet.

He braced himself, clenching his jaw. At this point his brothers would have shoved, and he'd have landed either on or too damn near the reptile.

Toni didn't shove. She squeezed his waist and said, "Brand, it's only a barn snake."

"What in the hell do you mean it's 'only a barn snake'? That SOB's six feet long." He wished he wasn't too busy to enjoy the press of her breasts against his back.

"He'll eat a lot of rats."

"Toni, I only have one rule about snakes. That a live one needs to be a dead one." Short of turning his back on the snake—which he would not do—and tossing Toni over his shoulder, there was no way for him to get them both out of the barn. *And he wouldn't leave Toni behind.* That was as sobering a thought as he'd ever had. He'd risk a snake for Toni.

When Toni backed off, Brand exhaled. Now he could get out of here. His ego had taken a hit. He'd shown his yellow streak in front of his wife. He inched backward.

The stall door opposite him opened. Toni stood framed in the sunlight. "Shoo him my way, Brand."

"No way." His throat knotted again at the thought of putting her in danger. His heartbeat thundered in his ears.

"Brand, we need to get him out before the crew brings the horses back in for the night. Shoo him out the door."

"I want a shovel or a gun. I want him in pieces."

Toni stepped out of sight. The snake eyed Brand. It eyed the open door. He hoped like hell it chose the door. He'd embarrassed himself enough already without running for the exit.

Toni came in behind him and elbowed him aside. With nothing more than a broom she approached the monster, shooed him outside, then closed the stall door. Was she crazy? Brand found himself rigid with fury that she'd risk herself over a snake. He grabbed her shoulders and pressed her against the wall.

"Are you out of your freakin' mind?"

Eyes wide, Toni shrank away from him. He felt her trembling beneath his hands and didn't understand it. She'd shown no fear of the monster. Why was she shaking now that it was gone?

"It was a *snake*. A big snake. He could have bitten you."

"B-barn snakes don't b-bite." He released her, but she remained wary. "Our—our tack room is overrun with mice. A dozen barn snakes that size would be nice right about now. I've handled snakes much larger than that one before."

Brand's eyes bulged and his gut pitched. "You pick 'em up?"

She shrugged and put a couple of steps between them without talking her eyes off him. "It's my job. I specialized in large animals, but I studied everything else. I had a part-time job with a small-animal vet. He treated reptiles."

Brand suppressed a shudder. Once more, Toni's delicate image bit the dust. If the woman could handle snakes, she could handle anything. So why had she been shaking after the fact? She didn't give him time to ask.

"Why are you terrified of snakes?"

What was left of his ego curled up and died. He shoved his hands in his pockets and turned away. He wanted to spit or scratch or do one of those obnoxious guy things that proved he wasn't a sissy. But he didn't. He had a feeling Toni would see right through it. "You mean why am I a coward?"

"That's not what I asked. A lot of people are afraid of snakes, Brand. I'd say you were more than just afraid."

Brand scraped up a pile of shavings with his boot, then spread 'em back out. Toni waited. Resigning himself to telling the tale, Brand leaned against the stall.

"When I was six, my best friend and I were swimming in the creek. We knew we weren't supposed to swim after a hard rain, but we did anyway. He got into a moccasin bed and was bitten more times than you can count. He died. Right there on the bank."

A picture of Dan's punctured body flashed in his mind. As if it were yesterday, he could hear his best friend struggling for his last breath. A shudder racked him.

Toni curled an arm around his waist and she hugged him. *Hugged him.* He'd vowed that his kid would have hugs, but he didn't know how he was supposed to respond to one. He took a deep breath and cleared his throat. Tentatively, he put his arms around her waist. It felt right to be standing here in her arms in the dimly lit barn.

"Ever since I haven't…liked snakes much. My brothers knew it and used every opportunity to scare me. If there was a snake around, you can bet they'd catch it and put it somewhere for me to find. Boots, lunch boxes, toilet. You name it. Patrick was bitten when he tried to catch a rattler to torture me with. We weren't sure he'd pull through."

Toni gasped and tightened her arms. "That's horrible. Why would they do that?"

Brand shrugged. "They're my brothers. Brothers do that kind of thing for fun."

He'd expected ridicule, not compassion. Was Toni ever going to do what he expected? Brand studied his boots. "Toni, I'm sorry I embarrassed you at the bank today. I should have explained beforehand that I want to keep my rodeo business separate."

The sympathetic softness left her eyes. They went from the soft blue of a baby's blanket to the hard silvery blue of an ice chip. Her arms fell from his waist and she stepped away.

"You made your point, Brand. You don't trust me. I can't say I blame you. We've known each other less than two weeks, and I didn't exactly start off on the best foot. Just don't expect me to extend my trust to you when I'm getting nothing in return."

Brand watched her stomp off toward the bunkhouse. He'd let her go work with Roy. She needed time to cool down, and maybe by tonight he'd find the words to make her understand.

One thing was for sure, next time he had her curled against him he'd just shut up and kiss her.

Toni held the sink against the wall while Roy tightened a piece of pipe beneath it. The bunkhouse renovation was nearly complete. As far as she was concerned that wasn't good news.

"So how'd you lasso him?" Roy's question nearly caused her to drop the sink on his head.

"What?"

He cranked the socket wrench another time and heaved his bulk out from beneath the porcelain. "How'd you catch Brand? He never fools around during the season. Lives like a danged monk."

Toni squirmed inwardly, certain that if Roy heard the truth she'd have another crew that hated her guts. "I—I don't know. It just sort of…happened."

"You can let go now. It oughta hold." Roy scratched his head and plunked on his hat. "Ain't no secrets on the circuit, but nobody knew 'bout you 'cept Bobby Lee. An' all he'd say is you left Vegas and Brand hired somebody to find you."

He started packing away the tools. "Never thought Brand was the marrying sort. He's had a thing going with

some li'l gal—name of Megan, I b'lieve—at Coyote Western Wear, y'know, one of those sponsor companies, for
the last couple of years, but he's never been serious about
nobody.'' His gaze caught Toni's. ''Until he up and married you.''

Unexpected jealousy made it difficult to get a word out.
Toni gave herself a mental kick. She had no claim on
Brand prior to Vegas, and if she'd had her way, she
wouldn't have one on him now. *Liar.* All right, for some
reason the thought of Brand with another woman bothered
her. Unclenching her fingers from the basin, she tried to
sound unconcerned. ''He has a girlfriend?''

Roy snapped the latch on the toolbox and faced her.
''Last I heard, he did, and it wasn't you.'' He patted her
on the shoulder. ''Nothing for you to be worried about
since he put a ring on your finger. Brand ain't the cheatin'
kind. I'm heading out to help the boys.''

''Right. Nothing to worry about.'' Toni forced her lips
into a smile and sank down on the edge of the bed Aaron
and Deke had assembled that morning. Her husband had
a lover. She should be happy. No, *thrilled.* Certainly he'd
want to sell out and spend more time with her. This was
good news wasn't it?

Then why did it make her so…miserable?

A quick rap on the bedroom door drew Toni's gaze.
Brand entered, closed the door and locked it. His gaze
drifted over the skin bared by the sagging neckline of her
oversize sweatshirt. She yanked up the material, folded her
arms, and tried to ignore the prickle of awareness his slow
perusal caused. She focused instead on how much his distrust hurt.

The day had been long and unpleasant beginning with
the embarrassing scene at the bank and ending with the
news that Brand had a girlfriend the last couple of years.
Add in the call to her mother and the confrontation in the
barn and she wasn't up to more heartache now. She was

cranky and short-tempered and she just wanted to be left alone.

Toni turned away. After a minute, she heard the bathroom door shut. She was angry with Brand and even more with herself. The crew had told her so much about Brand's generosity over the last few days—things she should have known before going to bed with him and totally ruining her plan. If she'd tried, she couldn't have chosen a man less likely to turn his back on his child. She didn't want to like the man she'd married, but it was too late. Brand Lander was truly a nice guy who didn't deserve what she'd done to him.

The water stopped splashing in the sink and the door opened. She faced him. "Why didn't you tell me this job was putting food on the table for Aaron and Deke's huge family? Or that Roy is battling alcoholism and you offered him a job and a place to dry out?"

Brand wiped his face on a towel, looking a little uncomfortable. "They're my buddies, Toni. I'm helping out the only way I know how."

"And Wade? That poor kid's older brother used to get high and beat him up. He told me he ran away the day he turned eighteen and ended up with you. For him, you're like a father and hero rolled into one. He bends over backward to impress you."

Brand shrugged. "He's a good road partner. Likes to drive."

"So why didn't you just tell me instead of ramming your friends down my throat? Didn't you think I'd understand and back you one hundred percent?" She reached for him, but lowered her hand before making contact. Touching him would only complicate things. "You're doing a good thing, Brand."

She turned to stare at her reflection in the darkened window. She'd done her best to forget Vegas, had even tried blaming that crazy rush of sensation on hormones and alcohol. She knew she lied. From the moment she'd set eyes on Brand Lander, he'd mesmerized her. At the most inconvenient times she caught herself recalling his taste and the feel of his calloused fingertips skipping along her skin. In Brand's arms she'd felt womanly, wise and wonderful, not cold-blooded and calculating.

His gentleness and his obvious concern for her pleasure had shocked her. All her life, no one had ever cared enough to find out what made her tick. She'd gone looking for a bum and ended up with a man who anticipated her desires before she recognized them herself.

The gentle touch of his hands on her shoulders made her jerk in surprise. With his thumbs he pressed soothing circles along her spine and beneath her shoulder blades, untangling knots of tensions. She bit her lip, battling the urge to lean into him.

"I don't know how to be a husband, but I am working on it." Brand murmured the words against her nape, stirring the fine hairs along her neck and shoulders. Heat crackled down her spine and pooled in her abdomen. The man dissolved her good sense and made her want so much more than the solitary life she'd planned.

"Sex won't solve anything," she whispered. But heavens, he made her feel good. When Brand held her close, being female didn't mean being powerless or victimized. It meant an equitable giving and receiving of pleasure. In his arms, she had a power she'd found nowhere else. *And it didn't hurt.*

Brand turned her to face him. The hot promise in his eyes lured her, tempting her to take a risk. "Maybe not, but we have to start somewhere. Find some common ground with me, Toni."

He slid his hands down her arms and stroked a hypnotic pattern on her wrists, her palms. Tiny shocks of sensation radiated from his light caress to the pit of her stomach. With slow, deliberate movements Brand lifted her hands to his shoulders. He cupped her waist and feathered seductive, tender kisses along her hairline, her jaw. Her lids grew heavy.

This wasn't a good idea and she knew it. If she had half a brain she'd end this madness before it consumed her. It was important to keep her distance, because Brand would leave. Suddenly, it didn't matter. What mattered was now.

His teeth tugged her earlobe. Toni's breath hitched. He traced the shell of her ear with his tongue and her knees weakened. Afraid she'd collapse at his feet, she dug her fingers into his broad shoulders and let her head fall to the side. Brand took advantage by opening his mouth and swirling his hot tongue over her erratic pulse. He nuzzled her neck band aside and nibbled on her shoulder, her collarbone.

She was sinking fast into a white-hot pool of sensation, but some part of her sanity held on. "I won't share."

Brand drew back, confusion mingling with the desire in his gaze. "Share what, darlin'?"

"You."

The possessive flash in his dark eyes held her captive, and the sexy curl of his lips destroyed the last of her resistance. "You won't have to."

For a moment Toni battled her conscience, then she surrendered to her need to get closer to Brand. Her eager fingers fumbled with the buttons of his shirt.

"Easy, darlin', we have all night." Brand's hands swept beneath her baggy sweatshirt, skimming up over her ribs to cup her bare breasts. The calloused pads of his thumbs scratched erotically over her pebbled nipples with a touch so delicate it nearly made her weep. Had it not been for his strong thigh thrust between her own, she might have sunk to the floor in a mindless puddle of need.

Brand whisked her shirt over her head, scooped her up. He carried her to the bed and set her down in the middle of the mattress. He left her long enough to yank off his shirt, then he knelt over her again. The crisp curls on his chest tickled her breasts like a thousand tiny fingers while he finger-combed her hair across the coverlet.

"When I close my eyes at night I see you like this."

He captured her surprised gasp with his lips, kissing her long, slow, deep, as if he had all night to devote to making love to her mouth. With his tongue, he explored the recesses and invited her to do the same to his. Toni accepted the invitation. She tested the softness of his lips, tasted the silky cavern. He closed his lips around her tongue and sucked. Rational thought fled. Her fingers were hungry for the satiny skin and taut muscles of his back. Clasping her thighs around his, she arched shamelessly against the ridge of his arousal, fitting him tighter to her aching center.

Brand reared back with a sharply indrawn breath. "Whoa, darlin'. Don't rush it."

He lowered his head and nuzzled her breast with the rough stubble of his chin, then followed it up with the silky, slick heat of his tongue. When he suckled her deep into his mouth, Toni could only moan and dig her fingers into his hair as the vortex of pleasure pulled her under. He licked and nibbled his way across her abdomen to the opposite breast. Her blood became lava. Her heart pounded harder in an effort to push the thick liquid through her veins.

Brand tugged the sweatpants from her and nuzzled the sensitive skin on the inside of her thighs. In Vegas, he'd shown her exquisite pleasure with his intimate kisses. He'd made her lose control and she hadn't minded. Tonight was no different. Desire curled and tightened, centering all her thoughts, all her feelings, on the stroke of his tongue. She clutched his hair, his shoulders, the sheets, as he brought her to peak after peak, not stopping until she whimpered, "No more."

His husky chuckle vibrated against her belly like the purr of a cat. "Oh, darlin', we have barely even started. Undress me."

It was only then that she realized Brand still wore his

jeans and boots. She felt a moment's embarrassment over
her nakedness, but he gave her time for no more than that
before he scorched her with another hot kiss. When they
broke for air she scooted down the bed, anxious to get him
bare. She grasped a boot and tugged, but it didn't budge.

"Stand at the foot of the bed," he instructed, his voice
rusty and full of promise. Toni slid off the bed, eager to
do anything he suggested if it meant getting him naked,
getting him inside her. "Now turn around."

Never crazy about the width of her bottom, she hesitated, but the fire in his eyes told her to risk the exposure.
She turned and saw the stranger from Vegas in the mirror
on the dresser, a wanton woman with disheveled hair and
glowing eyes. Whisker burn marked her breasts, her neck,
her thighs. Brand's tanned hands framed her waist. His
boot appeared between her legs.

"Now bend over and pull," he instructed. Toni grasped
the boot and felt the sole of the other on her bare buttock.
He pushed, she pulled. The boot came off in her hands.
She tugged off his sock and tossed it away. Brand switched
legs, and she repeated the procedure.

She tried to turn. His hands tightened on her hips and
held her in place. The warmth of his breath brushed over
her sensitized skin. He pressed kiss after kiss over her
rounded behind. His lips held her captive, marking an upward trail on her vertebrae as he stood to shove off his
jeans. He kicked them aside and sat back down. Brand
pulled her back, opening her legs over his. Suddenly,
swiftly, unexpectedly, his arousal filled her, pushing the
air from her lungs and all thought from her mind.

"Ride me, Toni." Rough words, groaned against her
back, sent an electric charge to her womb. She caught
Brand's reflection in the mirror. Streaks of color swept his
cheekbones. His eyes were closed and his jaw clenched.
His Adam's apple bobbed. His hot, harsh breath blew
against the fine hairs on her skin. Each follicle acted like
a lightning rod, accepting a charge and relaying it until her

body hummed like a tuning fork. He lifted his lids and the heat of his dark chocolate eyes melted over her.

As if feeling his possession wasn't erotic enough, Toni saw it all in the mirror. Brand shoved her hair over one shoulder and buried his mouth against her neck. She saw it coming, but nothing could prepare her for the sensual prickle of his evening beard or the scorch of his tongue. She witnessed tanned hands cupping her pale breasts, rolling her peaked nipples and it multiplied her response tenfold. His hands stroked downward, spreading her pale thighs wider. Golden curls mingled with nearly black. Then his biceps bunched in a raw display of power as he lifted and lowered her. She saw herself, open and vulnerable to his possession.

And she wasn't afraid.

Planting her feet on the floor, Toni lifted then lowered, following the rhythm Brand demonstrated with a firm grip on her waist. One of his big, scarred hands parted her feminine folds to caress the heart of her with a touch so delicate it amazed her. Her blood sluiced through her veins. Her heartbeat nearly deafened her. Before her eyes, her body swallowed his length while his hands stroked her magically. *Gently.*

The thick muscles in his arms and legs contracted. Instead of the fear she expected, the strength of his body fascinated her. She couldn't resist tracing the raised veins on his forearms to the backs of his hands. When she dragged her nails lightly over his thighs, Brand bowed his back and smothered a groan against her neck. He nipped her shoulder, his face tightening, as if he were in agony.

But he didn't hurt her.

Even lost in the throes of passion he was careful. He bucked again, nearly unseating her, and surged into her harder, faster. And together they watched his body, slick with her dew, sliding into hers again and again.

Lightning struck. The tingles began at her toes and shot upward in a shower of sparks. She jerked against him, her back arching. His arms tightened around her, but never to the point of pain. She heard Brand groan her name, felt his own cataclysmic explosion. And then all was still except for the sound of their labored breathing.

Slowly, Toni's heart rate approached normal. Her thighs ached and her body felt tender. She couldn't have supported her own weight. She sagged into the heat of Brand at her back and looked at the two of them in the mirror. How could she find such abandon in a man's arms, and how could she trust a man so lost in passion not to injure her? But she did. She trusted Brand and she was afraid she might be falling in love with him.

His chin rested heavily on her shoulder, and his chest still heaved. He met her gaze in the mirror and a drowsy smile quirked the corner of his mouth. Keeping her anchored against him with one hand, he used the other to brush the hair from her eyes and stroke a droplet of sweat from her cheek.

"Darlin', if we're half as good at running a ranch together as we are at this, the Rockin' A will be the best damned spread in the country."

Toni felt her lips curl in a sad smile. If only it were that easy. She'd finally found a man she could trust not to hurt her physically and he had the power to destroy her mentally by taking away the most important thing in her life— her sanctuary.

"I'm behind you, Toni." His tone implied more that just his present physical location. "We can make this work. I don't know how, but we will."

Brand helped her to her feet, turned her to face him, and pulled her between his thighs. His eyes were intent as he dragged a knuckle along her jaw. "I'll help you get this place the way you want it to be, but you have to work with me, not against me."

The pad of his finger drifted from her collarbone to her nipple. Formulating a reply took too much effort. "It's difficult to work with you when you're the only one who knows what you're doing.''

Brand nodded. "Tomorrow, after we set the men to work, you and I'll sit down and talk. The bull pen can wait until after lunch."

Toni bristled at the reminder. "I don't like bucking bulls."

Brand sighed. "I can walk away from competing, Toni, but I can't just toss out years of my life. I've learned a hell of a lot, and I want to share it with the kids coming up."

Toni understood goals. Vet school had been one step toward her goal of independence. "I did a lot of work in animal husbandry in school specifically with the goal of trying to crossbreed for leaner beef. I don't know anything about raising bucking stock."

"But that's what I do know." Brand's hand stroked the skin between her navel and her tight golden curls. "What about our breeding stock? When will you know?"

As if his hand were a magnet, the iron in her blood pooled beneath the warmth of his palm, distracting her from the determined tone of his voice. "Another week or so, I guess."

His eyes held hers. "I want to know as soon as you do."

Toni swallowed the knot in her throat. Was it caused by fear or longing? She didn't know. What she did know was that the thought of carrying Brand's baby, of being tied to this man for the rest of her life through a child, didn't terrify her the way it once had. "Okay."

He yawned hugely. "Right now, I want to curl up next to you and get some sleep. You've worn me out, darlin'." He winked then bent forward to suckle her nipple. "Course, it might take me a while to get to sleep."

Eight

Brand heard the truck long before he saw it.

He tightened another bolt in the section of the metal bullring he and the crew were assembling. Toni was up on the roof of the barn, determined to reshingle it herself. Short of putting his foot down and hiding the ladder, he hadn't had a choice but to let her do the job. Nobody in town was interested in working on the Rocking A. Wade was afraid of heights. Roy was just too damn big and awkward to be that far off the ground. Aaron and Deke were the only ones who knew how to install a bull fence.

The old El Camino rust bucket came to a shuddering halt beside the ring. The engine backfired and Toni squealed. Brand's blood ran cold. With his heart in his throat, he spun toward the barn, expecting to see her tumbling from the roof. Instead she skidded from the apex on her behind, clambered down the ladder at breakneck speed and sprinted across the yard to launch herself at the driver of the truck.

Beau came out of the barn howling as if in mortal pain. Brand glanced away from Toni long enough to make sure the dog hadn't been bitten by that damned barn snake. The mutt streaked toward the newcomer. It was the first time Brand had seen the dog move faster than a snail.

The man climbing from the truck not only looked like Santa Claus, his booming laugh sounded like him, too. Toni wrapped her arms around their visitor's wide middle and gave him a hug. Beau squirmed and wiggled beside them like an overeager puppy.

Brand put down his tools and headed in their direction. That burn in his gut was hunger, not jealousy. So the guy made Toni laugh. Big deal. And Beau liked him. So what?

The visitor's light blue eyes glittered a warning as Brand approached. The closer he got, the stiffer the man's spine became and the more his chest swelled.

"This the one?" When Toni nodded, the Santa impostor planted his broad self in front of Brand and glared. "You been messin' with my girl?"

The guy had him by at least sixty pounds, but Brand had him beat by a few inches in height, not to mention thirty years or so. Brand glared right back. "You talking about my wife?"

Toni squeezed between them. "Rusty, this is Brand Lander. Brand, Rusty Jackson, Granddad's old foreman."

"Watch who you're calling old, gal." The warmth in the man's pale blue eyes when he looked at Toni softened the harsh words. They turned back to ice before settling on Brand.

Toni smiled at the old man, her love clear for all to see. It hit Brand hard. She hadn't smiled at him like that. Not even after last night. The realization that he wanted her to winded him.

"Brand, Rusty's here to help us turn this place around." She clutched his forearm and squeezed. The look in her eyes told him how important his response was to her.

Brand looked at Toni then at Jackson and back to Toni. "You've hired him to be foreman?"

Toni took a deep breath and tilted her chin. "Yes."

Maybe they should've talked this morning after all, but they'd sent the crew off and gone back to bed. He wondered if she would have told him about the old man. She'd hired someone without consulting him, exactly as he'd done to her. He didn't like it any better than she had, but he remembered her words about trusting. It stung him to do so, but Brand offered his hand. "Welcome."

The man's shoulders relaxed. "Thanks."

"The men finished the bunkhouse this morning. Let's move in your gear." His acceptance of the new foreman earned him one of Toni's smiles. He grabbed the back of her neck and pulled her forward to plant a hard kiss on her lips. "That all right?"

She hugged him then saluted, clicking the heels of her boots together. "Yes, sir."

Toni was frisky and happy. He didn't know if he'd ever seen a more lethal combination. And she'd hugged him again. He could get used to that. Although he wanted to linger over her smiling lips, he turned away and grabbed a suitcase from the bed of the truck. He led Rusty to the bunkhouse. Toni followed.

"Choose your bunk."

"Toni didn't tell you about me?"

Brand sensed wariness in the old man's attitude, despite all his blustering outside. Before he could answer, Toni did. "Not yet."

"I can do the work. What I can't do I can explain real well, so's the younger ones can learn. I may be old, but there's a lot of life stored up here." Rusty tapped his head.

"There's easier jobs than ranching," Brand pointed out.

Rusty nodded. "Yeah, but there ain't no challenge in handing out smiley stickers and shoppin' carts at SuperMart." Toni patted his arm.

Jackson and his father were about the same age. He

didn't think his dad would survive without the ranch. "Did you and Toni agree on a salary?"

The man's cheeks flushed. He and Toni shared a grimace. "I was so danged glad to hear from her, I didn't think to ask. I just quit my job and packed my gear." Rusty looked at his scuffed boots.

Brand's gaze followed. He'd seen his dad in broken-down boots, and he'd put a stop to it as soon as he'd started earning serious money.

"What did Toni's grandfather pay you?"

Rusty named a pitifully low figure. Brand managed to conceal his wince, but Toni didn't. Even five years ago that was low. Brand named a figure more in keeping with the current market. "There'll be health insurance in addition to that and a bonus if we turn a profit."

Relief flashed in the man's eyes. "You won't regret it, Mr. Lander. I'll earn every penny." It was worth every cent he'd pay the man to see the approval in Toni's eyes.

"Call me Brand. Mr. Lander is my dad. What size boots do you wear?"

Rusty looked away, red scorching his cheeks, but mumbled his size.

Toni looked uncomfortable. "Brand, I—"

"You wear the same size as me. I have a sponsor who gives me about two dozen pairs of boots a year. If you'd test-drive a pair or two for me I'd appreciate it. Let me know what you think of 'em, and I'll pass the word on to the manufacturers."

Rusty studied Brand for a moment as if trying to decide whether it was a legitimate offer or charity. He glanced at Toni and she shrugged. "All right. Long as you don't make me wear none of those funny-looking ones." He pointed to Brand's hand-tooled ostrich boots.

"Can't talk you into a red pair, can I?"

"Not while I'm still breathin'. I ain't no poster boy."

There were days Brand felt the same way, but he wore what he was paid to wear. The money was putting food on his family's table and paying Cort's tuition at one of the finest medical schools in the country. Sure, he could wear regular boots and clothes when he wasn't making public appearances, but it seemed stupid to waste money buying something he already had.

"We'll leave you to get settled." Capturing Toni's hand he led her outside. She glanced at him quizzically as he led her across the yard.

"Inside."

She nodded and continued toward the house.

In the kitchen she faced him. "I'm sorry. I should have told you I'd called Rusty, but after yesterday at the bank...I just needed someone on my side."

He was sorry his distrust had hurt her, but what was a man supposed to do? He had to protect what was his or risk losing it all the way Caleb had. His brother's wife had cleaned out the family's savings before leaving town. "Is he the right man for the job?"

Toni bit her lip. "Granddad swore Rusty was the best foreman in the state, but he had to leave about five years ago to take care of his brother who was dying from lung cancer."

Brand pulled her into his arms. She'd surprised him again with her concern for others. Obviously, Rusty needed the job as much as she needed him here. "Next time, we hire as a team. Now let's go introduce the foreman to his temporary crew.

"We'll set the men to work, and then we'll come back inside—" he waggled his brows "—and take a nap."

From the flush spreading across her cheeks, Brand knew she understood that sleep was the last thing on his mind. Even though he ought to be working on his bull pen, he'd rather spend the next hour holding Toni than holding a wrench. The thought worried him for about two seconds. When Toni's gaze heated and her lips curved with sensual promise he forgot about his bulls. Wrapping an arm around her shoulders, he nibbled her earlobe, and whispered what he wanted to do with her. Once Toni's face was as flushed as his felt, Brand led her outside.

Brand forked another load of fluffy omelet into his mouth and passed Toni the plate of Texas toast. Rusty Jackson was one heck of a cook.

"I carried the boys' breakfast out to the bunkhouse." Rusty set himself down with a heaping breakfast.

Toni huddled over her coffee cup as if eight hours of uninterrupted sleep could be found within the strong brew. Her lids were heavy, her lips slightly puffy. Buttery curls hung over her shoulders, reminding him of how they'd felt dragging across his chest last night. She'd never looked sexier. He wanted her. Again.

He squeezed her knee beneath the table and traced the seam of her jeans along the length of her thigh. He loved watching the color rise in her cheeks.

What had she done to him to make him want to forget everything except the feel and taste of her? Right now he didn't give a horse's behind about what was going on outside the ranch house. He wanted to grab his wife and drag her back upstairs. If he had his way they wouldn't see the light of day for weeks. That could be a serious problem. When a man started thinking with something besides his head he stood a good chance of taking a nasty toss, but he figured the intense sexual attraction was a temporary thing. Might as well enjoy it for the short while it lasted.

Of course, Toni had other plans. She'd dragged him out of bed for this little meeting. "Rusty, you're more familiar with the limitations of the land than either Brand or me. We'd like to run some ideas by you." Toni glanced Brand's way. He winked.

Beneath the table Toni caught his hand and transferred it back to his own thigh. Brand refused to release her, and he knew she wouldn't struggle and risk Rusty catching on to the shenanigans beneath the table. He pressed her fingers to his thigh and gave her a smug smile.

She blushed and turned back toward Rusty. The fighting angle of her chin should've warned Brand that he wasn't in control of the situation. Her hand under the table wreaked havoc with his concentration. She pulled her thumb free and scratched her fingernail over the worn denim beneath his fly. His temperature skyrocketed and his brain short-circuited when his blood headed south. He and Toni were great together in bed, but she'd never initiated anything before.

She smiled sweetly, but he saw the mischief in her eyes and the flush staining her neck. "I trust you to be unbiased."

"Gal, just cause I nearly wore you in my hip pocket for years, don't mean I'll let you run the place into the ground."

"I studied genetics in vet school with the intention of raising a crossbreed of cattle that's leaner than the strand Granddad was running. The Rocking A has always been a beef-cattle operation." She made a circle over a particularly sensitive area. Brand tried to steady his breathing.

Rusty nodded. "That it has."

Brand tried and failed to focus on the complicated genetic discussion going on while Toni explained her research. What she proposed would take years of measuring and charting the changes in the herd. He didn't expect her to be around long enough to see it through, and he didn't have the training or the inclination to take over once she left.

He pressed his thighs together, trapping her troublemaking fingers. He needed a clear head if he planned to win this argument. "Beef prices are down. It'd be more profitable to raise bucking bulls. Rodeo's hotter than ever. Demand's up. I also want to open a rodeo school. I'll need to add on an arena and access roads that'll eat into your pasture space."

Her hand stilled. There was genuine concern in Toni's

eyes and voice. "Wouldn't you have to demonstrate to teach?"

Other than Cort, his own family never seemed concerned with the risks he took to put money in their bank account. Did she actually care if he got hurt? Her life would be easier with him out of the picture.

He laced his fingers with hers. "Toni, it's my job. I'm damned good at it."

She pulled free and stood. "It doesn't matter how good you are, Brand. Accidents happen all the time—especially around unpredictable bulls. You could be injured or...or worse. Would you want to leave your child without a father?"

The fluffy eggs turned to bricks in his stomach. The woman fought dirty. "We don't know if there is a baby yet."

"We don't know there's not."

Her earnest blue eyes wrenched his heart. His gaze dropped to her flat belly. Would his plans change if he had a son or a daughter? Would he risk never seeing his child ride a pony or a school bus? He'd been the one to break the news to his buddy's wife and two small kids when his buddy had been pronounced dead at the scene of a rodeo wreck. Would he put his kid through that? He felt his dream and his promise slipping from his grasp.

"I can do most of the work from the ground."

Rusty held a hand up, stifling Toni's protests. "Not ever' man is as careless as Josh Keegan was, Toni. His mind was on courtin' you, not on what he was doing.

"The boy got hisself gored 'bout ten years ago," he said to Brand. "Didn't think he'd pull through. You'll have to promise Toni-girl you'll hire bullfighters, wear flak jackets and not take stupid chances."

His gaze holding Toni's, Brand nodded. "I'll be careful."

"Missy." Rusty pointed a finger toward Toni. "You didn't tell me there might be a young'un on the way. If there is, your job's gonna change. None of that roof climbing, for starters.''

Toni sputtered. Brand sat back and let the old man lecture.

"Now you, cowboy.'' Brand stiffened. "There's plenty of land on the Rocking A, and you ought to have enough money to set Toni up and have your bulls, too. Let her do her work while you do yours.''

"You're suggesting we run a dual operation?''

"Don't see why not.''

"All right. Toni'll have her business and I'll have mine.'' Dividing the ranch down the middle wasn't what he had in mind, but at least he'd have control over his half of the ranch.

Toni smiled. It slammed Brand with the force of a bull's kick. He found himself grinning foolishly back. He liked making her smile. Not just any smile, but *that smile,* the one that put sparkles in her eyes and a spring in her step.

He knew better than to become attached. His head knew she'd leave, but his heart didn't seem to be getting the message. He kept thinking about what would happen if Toni stayed—the ranch they'd share, the kids they'd have. It wasn't something he'd ever considered with any other woman, and he wasn't real happy to be thinking about it now. Sooner or later, reality was gonna kick him in the teeth.

Toni's brow furrowed. "Is something wrong?'' Brand couldn't speak past the tightness in his throat, so he just shook his head. "Then why are you still here? Aren't your bulls due at the train station in an hour or so? You should have left already.''

His bulls. He needed his head examined for letting a woman come between him and work. "Yeah, I need to go…Toni, stay away from the bulls, all right?''

She stiffened and the sparkle faded from her eyes. "You don't trust me with your money *or* your bulls?''

Brand silently cursed his clumsy tongue. "No, I don't

want you to be hurt. You said yourself they're unpredictable. Besides, you don't like 'em.''

She was all starch and fire, poker-straight back and flashing eyes. "I have news for you, Brandon Lander. As the only vet on this ranch, I'll be very close to those bulls and any other livestock on the Rocking A. It's my job and I'm good at it.''

She threw his own words back in his face. He slid his hand from her waist to cup her stomach. "If you won't think about you, think about the baby.''

She took a step back and hugged her arms across her chest. Her face paled. "You couldn't possibly believe I'd do something to harm my child.''

He needed to keep his mouth shut. Every time he opened it, he made things worse. He grabbed his hat and headed for the door. "I need to go, or I'll be late.''

"Brand? Be careful.'' Concern clouded her eyes and she gnawed her lip.

He winked and made a crossing motion over his heart, the gesture of the carefree cowboy he'd been before he met Toni.

Despite what people said, bull riding was a thinking man's game, and usually he was a thinking man. From the moment he'd met Toni he'd deviated from that course, acting and reacting from his gut and not his head. That had to change.

Toni propped her chin on a rail and wondered why Brand had married her on the mere possibility of a child when he could have waited just a few short weeks to be sure. What were the odds that she'd conceived?

She'd thought they had something growing between them, a relationship that might be worth holding on to, until today when the blinders had fallen off. Brand was protective, but not of her. He was concerned for the maybe baby. He wanted her to stay off the barn roof, off the windmills, off the horses' backs and away from the bulls. The list grew daily and it chafed.

Because of the baby. She was a fool. She'd felt cherished when his only concern was for a child that might not even exist. Where would that leave her if she weren't pregnant? Would he leave? Toni's throat tightened. Wasn't having the ranch to herself what she wanted? Now that Brand had agreed to fund her vision of the ranch and keep his own business separate she wasn't sure anymore. It'd be like dividing the property into His and Hers sectors. That common ground he talked about would be limited to the bedroom. She wanted more than just great sex.

She shoved away from the fence. Like it or not, the bulls were on their way and she needed to get ready for them.

She'd just finished filling the water troughs when Brand's truck, towing a long stock trailer, turned into the driveway. Another pickup followed close behind. Toni opened the bull-pen gate and watched Brand back the trailer toward the opening. Nerves knotted in her stomach. Dread stiffened her muscles.

She stared through the iron bars on the side of the stock trailer. A brindle bull occupied the front section, separated from his traveling companion by a hinged divider. The bull in the rear was big, black and ugly. He snorted in her face and charged the bar. Toni jumped back. Bulls had always frightened her—especially after Josh's accident. But Rusty was wrong. It hadn't been her Josh had been trying to impress. He'd been more interested in one of the ranch hands. Josh was gay. But that wasn't her secret to tell.

Brand unlatched one side of the loading ramp. Toni tightened her fingers on the metal gate. She knew she should be helping him unload the beasts, but her feet wouldn't move. She kept seeing Josh flying through the air. She remembered the dust mingling with blood on the ground. Then the picture blurred and it was Brand in the dirt.

Before she could unlock her knees, Craig Stevens, the

local vet, appeared beside her and reached to unlock the side of the ramp nearest to her.

"Hi there, Toni. I ran into Brand in town and came out to look over these bad boys for myself, but I want to talk to you before I leave." Dr. Stevens returned his attention to the restless animals in the trailer. He popped the latch and yelled, "Got it."

The black bull exploded from the trailer, bucking and kicking. Toni screamed a warning to Brand and the bull turned toward her. A hoof connected with the gate and pain exploded her shins, her chest and her forehead. She found herself lying flat on her back in the dirt.

Before she could catch her breath, Brand knelt over her. "Are you all right?"

A shaft of pain shot through her head when she nodded.

"Don't move your head." Brand's hands gently traced her skull then cupped her face. "Tell me where you're hurtin'."

"I...I'm okay. Just winded, I think." She wiped her brow. Warm, sticky blood covered her hand.

Dr. Stevens jumped to his feet. "I'll get some sterile bandages out of the truck."

With one hand, Brand pressed his bandanna to her wound. His other hand swept across her abdomen. His eyes, darkened with concern, held hers. Her heart contracted at the emotion she saw there. "Are you sure you're okay?"

Her head cleared as if he'd dumped ice water over her. The pain in her skull dulled in comparison to the stabbing pain in her heart. Brand's only concern was for a baby that might not even exist. Embarrassed that she'd read him so wrong, she shoved his hand away, clambered to her feet, and nearly bit off her tongue as pain ricocheted through her. Her head spun. It hurt to breathe. She didn't know which injury ached most. But that was nothing. Her heart was breaking.

Brand grabbed her arm. Toni jerked away. She winced

and bent over at the spear of pain the sudden movement caused.

"Where you hurt, Toni-girl?" Rusty tried to elbow Brand aside but Brand wouldn't budge.

"I'm okay." His stern look warned her not to lie. Toni straightened. Carefully. "The gate caught my rib cage. Just a bruise, I think."

Brand supported her with an arm around her waist. "She got hit pretty hard. Knocked her clear off her feet. She needs a doctor. Let's go." Brand herded her toward her car.

"Brand, please. You're making too much of this."

Without a word, he swept her into his arms and carried her toward the car. He didn't stop until he set her down beside the door. "We're getting you to the hospital whether you like it or not, so stop arguing."

The pallor of his face and the genuine concern in his eyes halted any arguments she might have had. She sat down and he bent over her to buckle her belt. "I'm going to lay your seat back."

Brand gently peeled off the blood-soaked bandanna and studied her wound. His hands were shaking when he took an alcohol pad from Dr. Stevens and cleaned the cut. It stung like crazy and she flinched, but through the pain she realized Brand cared.

"Sorry, but I'm not risking an infection." He covered the cut with gauze squares and pressed her hand to the makeshift bandage. "Put pressure on it." She did as he said, but still he didn't move away.

"What's wrong?"

He shook his head. "Nothing a few stitches won't fix, but they'll be hidden by your hair. No scar to mar that pretty face." Still, he lingered for a few more seconds before moving around to the driver's side of the car.

The vet appeared. "You okay?"

"Just dented."

"Good. Because I'm short of help and I came over today to ask you to help me in my practice until that boy of mine graduates in June.''

"No," Brand said from the behind the wheel.

Toni jerked her head toward him, wincing as pain lanced her. "He was asking me."

"And you're in no shape to be talking about taking any more risks."

"Call me next week," she told the vet. She wouldn't let Brand dictate to her.

Nine

Brand took her to the hospital emergency room. When Toni's lack of health insurance threatened to slow things down, he whipped out his platinum charge card and passed it to the harassed clerk.

"Just get her a doctor." The nurse hastened to obey. "There's no point in trying to convince her you're covered by my plan when we don't have a card yet."

"I—I am?"

He nodded. "I added you the day after we got married."

She shouldn't have been surprised because Brand was always taking care of somebody. Now it was her turn. Did it mean she truly meant something to him? Or was she just another obligation?

A nurse showed her to a tiny curtained cubicle. She poked and prodded and asked innumerable questions, most of which were extremely personal and embarrassing, considering there was only a thin curtain and a half-dozen feet between her and the beds on either side of her. Her answers could be heard by at least ten people—including the man beside her.

The female physician was patient and thorough. "Any chance you might be pregnant?"

"Yes," Brand answered immediately.

"How far along?"

"Two weeks." Again Brand responded before Toni could.

The doctor raised her eyebrows in Toni's direction for clarification. "What was the first day of your last period?"

Heat climbed Toni's cheeks, and she supplied the date. "I'm only a few days late. I—I haven't done the test yet."

"That's plenty of time for an accurate result. We can do a pregnancy test here, if you like. Then we'll know whether it's safe to x-ray you," the doctor offered with a smile. "I'd like to rule out rib fractures and a concussion."

For once, Brand didn't snap out an answer. Toni focused on him rather than her own building panic. She watched him swallow hard and tighten his grip on the bedrail until his knuckles turned white. He looked as nervous as she felt.

"Mrs. Lander?" the doctor prompted.

"O-okay," she croaked out. What would Brand do if she weren't pregnant?

After suturing the cut, the doctor promised to send in a lab tech and left. Brand thrust his hands into his pockets and turned away as soon as the curtain swished closed. His spine was stiff. "You win. The bulls are going back."

Toni's heart did a funny little two-step. She'd never had a man make sacrifices for her. "Why don't you tell me why the bulls are so important to you?"

He turned his back before she could decipher the expression on his face. "I made a promise."

"What kind of promise?"

"When I first started riding, a retired rider saw how bad I wanted to win. He didn't charge me a dime for lessons because he knew I couldn't afford it. His only request was that I give back. Do for some other kid what he'd done for me.''

He faced her. The sadness in his eyes made Toni catch her breath. "Every year after the season is over I volunteered at his ranch, teaching the way he taught me. He had a stroke last spring, and he's pretty bad off. There won't be a camp this year because his wife sold the ranch. Hell, if I'd known she wanted to sell I'd have bought it, but nobody told me until the deal was done.''

"Then sending the bulls back would be a mistake. I wish you'd told me, Brand.''

He spun to face her. "I don't want you getting hurt again.''

Toni searched his eyes, hoping that he meant her and not just the baby she might be carrying. "I was hurt because I made a stupid, rookie mistake. I took my eyes off the animal. It wasn't your fault.''

Brand paced the small cubicle. The pain in Toni's head and shin subsided to a dull throb, and her rib only hurt when she breathed. Her stomach however was a different story. She was worrying herself into an ulcer.

"Brand, sit down and tell me why you chose rodeo in the first place.''

He hesitated before sinking into the chair beside her bed. "I didn't choose it as much as it chose me. I'd done some riding in high school and won some here and there, but I didn't plan to take it any further. I wanted to go to college.''

"What stopped you?''

"Before she left, Caleb's wife spent every dime we had—including my college money. Riding and *winning* was the only way to hold on to the ranch. Lucky for me I won more than I lost. Still, I didn't start winning fast enough. We had to sell half the ranch to keep from losing the whole spread.''

"Oh Brand, I'm sorry.''

He shrugged it off. "No big deal. Worked out for the best."

The doctor opened the curtain. "Congratulations. You're going to be parents."

Toni's heart nearly beat its way out of her chest. Her gaze met Brand's. His stunned expression no doubt matched her own.

The doctor frowned. "You didn't plan this baby?"

Toni stayed focused on Brand. His face was pale, his eyes glassy. She thought he might pass out. She covered his hand with hers. "Yes, yes I did."

She was going to have Brand Lander's baby. Part of her wanted to laugh with joy. Another part was disappointed because now she'd never know who Brand wanted, her or their child.

Toni was going to have his child. Brand's chest felt tight—kind of like the panic attack a fellow rider had once described. If the baby was a boy, Toni wouldn't need him anymore. She could boot him off the ranch and keep it to herself. And he didn't want to go. Wouldn't go, dammit.

He choked back a curse. He had no idea when or how it had happened, but despite trying to keep his distance, he'd done the unthinkable. He'd fallen in love with his wife.

It could have been in Vegas where the gutsy little angel had stolen his heart. He'd been surprised by the steely determination in such a delicate-looking package.

It could be the way she worked with the crew. Sometimes those guys were as clumsy as the Three Stooges in their attempts to impress her, but not once had she laughed at them.

Then there were the nights… Toni melted in his arms and made him feel like a god. The woman touched him or gave him that smile and he nearly exploded.

On automatic pilot, he helped her into the car and headed home. Damn. He hadn't intended to fall in love and didn't want to think about how he'd deal with it when she left or if she asked him to leave. Now he understood why his heart was in his throat each time she worked on the barn roof or scaled the windmills. If he kept the bulls, she'd insist on treating them. He didn't want to give them up or break his promise to his old friend, but he wasn't willing to put Toni at risk.

Brand scrubbed his hand across his face. He had a wife and now a kid on the way. Less than three weeks ago he'd had neither and hadn't wanted them. He felt as though a rogue bull had tossed him. Trampled. Stunned. And there were no bullfighters coming to his rescue. He was scared spitless.

Toni ached everywhere. With Brand's assistance she eased herself from the car. The ranch hands swarmed them. She was touched by their concern, but mostly she was worried because Brand hadn't said a word to her since the doctor had confirmed her pregnancy. As one, the group of men erupted into questions.

Toni held up her hands. "Just bruised. Relax."

"Let's get you settled inside," Brand said.

Toni looked at him and frowned. He was still as pale as a corpse. She let him lead her toward the house, in part because her head felt as if it were going to explode, but mostly because she needed time to think. *She was going to be a mother. Mission accomplished.* The reality of it terrified her. She was afraid she'd be as bad a parent as her own…or worse.

"You all right, Toni-girl?" At that moment, Toni thought Rusty looked every one of his sixty-two years.

"Just sore and embarrassed to have caused such a fuss, Rusty." She forced a smile for her mentor and squeezed his hand.

Some of the concern eased from his face. He nodded once, then focused a hard stare on Brand. "Your bulls are in the pen, but if they hurt my girl again, they're gonna be on the grill."

Brand didn't hesitate. "I like my steak medium rare."

Wade cleared his throat. "Ahh…Brand? Whatcha wanna do about that other thing in your truck?"

Toni watched Brand shake his head imperceptibly. Curious, she turned toward Wade and asked, "What other thing?"

Brand ran a finger under his collar, then hooked his thumbs through his belt loops. He glanced at her briefly then toward Rusty. "Nothing you need to worry about right now."

"No time like the present," she insisted, not liking the fact that Brand was keeping secrets again.

He seemed to consider her words, then huffed out a breath. "I bought you a four-wheeler. I'd rather you rode it than a horse if you have to go out into the pastures. You're less likely to fall off and hurt yourself or the baby."

Toni sucked a hasty breath as pain of a different sort lanced her. Her ribs protested. *The baby.* Again. His only concern was the baby. "The doctor said it was okay for me to pursue my normal activities."

His jaw jutted forward. "The doctor hasn't met that mare you insist on riding."

Toni sputtered with anger over Brand's high-handed attitude—even if he was right. She had no business on the back of that feisty horse when she was pregnant and she knew it. But to have him take the decision away from her reminded her too much of her past.

Aaron stepped forward before she could protest. "Wait a minute. Toni's pregnant? Hell, Brand, you didn't waste any time. You gonna keep her barefoot, too?"

Brand kept his eyes on Toni. "While you're angry, I might as well tell you I also bought cellular phones. I want you to take one wherever you go in case you have a problem. Rusty and I will each carry one."

"I am not a child who needs to be tracked every moment of the day," Toni snapped. "I'm not going to risk my baby or myself by doing something foolish. Credit me with a little sense, Brand."

"Toni-girl," Rusty stepped between them. His eyes held a wounded look. "This time I'm gonna side with Brand. Forty years ago I lost my wife and the baby she was carrying because she got throw'd from her horse and couldn't get help. She bled to death not two miles from the house. I'm not gonna stand by and let that happen to you when carrying a phone is so easy."

Anger instantly dissipated. Struggling with tears, she stepped into Rusty's embrace. She'd known him for years and she hadn't known this.

Toni met Brand's stoic gaze. "All right. I'll ride the four-wheeler and carry a phone." At least he wasn't trying to confine her to the yard the way her grandfather had. Yet.

Turning on her heel, Toni hobbled into the house. She didn't stop until she'd locked the bathroom door behind her. Turning on the taps, she peeled off her clothes as the tub filled. Already her shin, rib cage and forehead were turning colorful.

Toni sank into the warm water. She felt emotionally numb. Shell-shocked. Closing her eyes, she leaned her head back and let the warm water ease her aches. Would her baby have the melting Godiva-chocolate eyes of its daddy? That mischievous sparkle? The thick, nearly black hair with the recalcitrant curl on top? Would her son have the same swaggering step, the same broad shoulders?

What if it were a girl? Would she have her father's daredevil streak and the same tender heart? Toni stroked her still-flat belly. She knew she'd love a daughter just as much as a son, because it was a part of Brand. One thing she knew for sure, she'd never, *never* let anyone raise a hand to her child. Fingering the tiny horseshoe-shaped scar on her chin, Toni leaned back and closed her eyes. "I'll protect you," she murmured.

After a few words with the men, Brand followed Toni inside. He wanted to see her settled and comfortable. He'd left the ranch earlier without a thought of the bulls he'd been so eager to receive. His only concern had been for Toni. Now he knew why and he wanted to look in her eyes, knowing that he loved her. He wanted to touch her skin, knowing that he'd do anything to make her stay. He wanted to see if there was a fraction of his love reflected back in her gaze.

The closed bathroom door stopped him. Toni obviously wanted privacy and he couldn't blame her. His mind was reeling and his throat felt tight. *He was going to be a father.* He felt proud enough to strut and nervous enough to puke. He and Toni would have to talk, but later, when he'd had time to digest the news.

Back outside, he called the men together. "I'm gonna need your help keeping Toni from doing anything too strenuous. No roofing. No windmill climbing. No heavy lifting. And for Pete's sake, keep her away from the bulls."

Rusty cleared his throat. "You're making a mistake there, Brand. She ain't gonna like it if you try to corral her."

"I'm not corralling her, Rusty. I'm just trying to keep her from hurting herself."

"Her granddad said the same thing, and I'm telling you, you're gonna face a rebellion if you lay down the law. Toni's already told you she wouldn't do anything to hurt the baby. You gotta trust her. You won't have a marriage till you do."

The old man was right, but Brand couldn't trust Toni to look out for herself. There was too much at stake.

* * *

Toni rolled over, groaning as her multitude of bruises made their presence known. Brand's side of the bed was cold and empty. She hugged his pillow to her chest and inhaled his scent. Last night he'd shown her a gentleness she'd never experienced before. Did that make him different from her father?

Shoving back the covers, she stumbled into the bathroom and flinched at the sight of her battered face. Black, blue and purple covered the side of her forehead, stretching down to her cheekbone. Traces of blood still matted her hair. She looked as if she'd lost a barroom brawl. Even her father had never left her this bruised.

She couldn't camouflage this kind of disaster, and the doctor had told her to keep the cut dry. That meant washing the blood from her hair was out of the question.

Tugging on jeans and a sweatshirt, Toni went in search of something to settle her stomach. It felt a little off this morning. The smell of old coffee assaulted her as soon as she entered the kitchen. Her stomach revolted. Toni clapped a hand over her mouth and bolted for the bathroom. Holding her sore ribs with one hand and her hair with the other, she bent over the bowl. With each retch of her stomach, blistering pain burned through her side.

After rinsing her mouth and hands, Toni studied the battered, tear-streaked face in the mirror. A smile tugged at her lips. If she'd needed proof of her pregnancy, her antsy stomach was willing to provide it. She was going to have Brand's baby.

"Toni?"

She frowned, turning toward the voice. Surely that wasn't her mother? *Not now.* Toni stepped out of the bathroom. Her parents stood in the kitchen. "What are you doing here?"

Their horrified expressions stopped Toni in her tracks. Her face was a showstopper—worse than they'd seen before. Her hand covered the tender area. "I had a fight with a gate."

"A gate?" her father said with a sneer. Toni took a step back.

The kitchen door opened. Cool air and the scent of pine swept in, followed by Brand carrying a large Christmas tree. She'd been so caught up in getting pregnant, married, and renovating the ranch that she'd forgotten all about the upcoming holiday. Brand propped the pine against the wall and shut the door. "Oh, Brand. You bought a tree?"

"You the man who did this to my daughter?" Toni recognized the nuance in her father's voice. Before she could warn him, Brand grimaced and nodded. Freeing one hand from the tree, he offered it to her father. Her father plowed his fist into Brand's jaw. Brand dropped the tree and rocked back against the doorjamb, cupping his chin.

"What in the hell—"

"Daddy!" Horrified, Toni hobbled across the room. She knew the risk she took when she grabbed her father's arm as he drew back to hit Brand again. "Stop!"

"He hit you. I hit him." Toni had seen this side of her father before. He presented his public persona—smooth, suave, patience personified—until someone, usually his wife or daughter, made him angry. Then he lashed out.

Torn between fear of her father and the need to make sure Brand was all right, Toni's glance darted from one man to the other and back again. Brand had widened his stance, apparently ready to defend himself. Toni released her father's arm and stepped in front of Brand. She knew her father would just as soon hit her as anyone else. Tears of humiliation stung her eyes. Shame scorched her cheeks. She hadn't wanted to drag Brand into the sordid mess of her family. Now he knew her secret.

"I told you, Dad, I ran into a gate."

"Don't lie to me," he bellowed. Opening his palm, he drew back his arm. Toni clenched her jaw and braced herself for a blow.

With the swiftness of a striking snake, Brand caught her father's wrist, twisting it up and behind her father's back.

Her father groaned, but ceased his struggling when Brand yanked his arm up another notch. "Keep your damn hands off my wife."

"Nobody hits my daughter," her father threatened through gritted teeth.

"Nobody but you, you mean." The menace in Brand's voice made the hair on Toni's neck stand up. This was a side of him she'd never seen—no matter how hard she'd pushed. And she had pushed.

"Get your filthy hands off me," her father growled, struggling.

Brand yanked his wrist again. "You forgot to warn me about your father, darlin'. You all right?"

"I...you...I'm so sorry." Keeping a wary eye on her father, Toni studied the swelling area on Brand's jaw.

"Call the sheriff, Toni."

All her life, her father had acted out his anger with physical violence, but he'd never, to her knowledge, tried to hurt anyone besides her mother and herself. "Brand, he's my father."

"I don't care if he's your priest. He has no business hitting you. Call the sheriff."

Her mother grabbed her arm. "Don't, Toni, please."

Indecision twisted Toni's insides. The last time her father had hit her, she'd moved out the same night. She'd found a job and freedom, but guilt had burned like salt in an open wound because she'd left her mother behind. She'd known when she left that her mother would have no one to divert her father's anger.

"He needs help, Mom." She hadn't been able to save her mother then, but now... Toni reached for the phone.

"He's been getting help. He's doing better, I promise. He hasn't... We haven't had an incident in over a year."

"Until today," Brand muttered.

"Yes, well, it was a shock for Paul to find out Toni had married and then to see her so...bruised."

Brand flattened his lips. "There's never an excuse to beat up on a woman or someone smaller than you."

"Please, Toni, put down the phone. He's seeing a therapist every week." Her mother's plea made Toni lower the receiver.

The back door opened and Rusty stepped inside. "Came to help with the tree. Miss Allison, Mr. Paul, how're you—" Rusty studied the situation and frowned. "What's going on here?"

"My father thinks Brand is a wife beater, so he—"

Rusty shook his head slowly and said, "You're a real jackass, Swenson. Wassamatter? Don't want anybody else beatin' up on your women?"

Toni's father struggled and cursed Rusty. Brand jerked on his arm. He clamped his lips shut and paled.

"You can let him go, Brand," Rusty stated. "If he takes another swing at anybody, he knows I'll take him out. Been wantin' to for a damned long time."

Brand released Paul Swenson with obvious reluctance. "He needs to be locked up."

Her father huffed, straightened his jacket, and put as much space between himself and Brand as the room would allow. Toni kept her distance.

"Won't do any good." Rusty shook his head again. "Allison'll just bail him out. If she don't, the courts'll let him go."

"He's getting help," her mother insisted a third time.

"It doesn't seem to be working." Brand crossed the room to stand beside Toni.

Toni watched him carefully. He bristled with anger, but his eyes and the arm he looped around her waist were nothing but gentle. Cautiously, she stroked her fingers over his swelling jaw. "You need an ice pack."

He covered her hand with his. The understanding she found in his gaze made her eyes tear.

"Exactly how did my daughter get that black eye,

Rusty?'' her father asked. "And don't feed me any of that gate garbage."

"Toni don't lie," Rusty said, rummaging through the freezer. He offered an ice-filled plastic bag to Brand. Reluctantly, Toni released Brand and let him apply the ice.

"Ya don't have to worry about Brand, Miss Allison. I'll take out any man who hurts that girl myself," Rusty assured her mother. He shot a hard look toward Brand and then her father to make sure the warning was received.

Toni rolled her eyes. "I can take care of myself."

Her mother asked, "Why were you crying when you came out of the bathroom?"

Toni pulled in a shaky breath and glanced at Brand. You couldn't keep secrets around here. Although she would have liked to keep this one a little longer. Say…nine months or so. "I wasn't crying. I'd had my first bout with morning sickness. Brand and I are going to have a baby."

If the news of her hasty marriage had surprised them, then news of her pregnancy shocked them. Her father looked ready to take another swing at Brand.

Brand turned her in his arms and brushed a hand across her cheek. "You all right?"

"The smell of stale coffee upset my stomach, but I'm okay." Without a word, Brand crossed the room, grabbed the pot, and emptied it into the sink.

"Toni, you had no business getting married without letting us meet him first." Her father said *him* with enough emphasis to make a less confident man cringe. "You know nothing about men—"

"I know enough to know which kind to avoid." Her father bristled. Toni reminded herself it was best not to provoke him, but some habits were hard to break.

"He's a rodeo bum."

Brand leaned against the counter and studied his in-laws. His jaw hurt. The ice bag was cold. And his heart was breaking. Now that he knew Toni's secret, he wished he didn't. Thoughts of the bastard smacking her around brought out a violence he hadn't known he possessed. If Rusty hadn't walked in, Brand knew he probably would have broken Paul Swenson's arm. Then his face.

Toni's father was a tall man, a couple of inches over Brand's six feet, and whipcord lean. Brand could forgive him for taking a swing at him because he thought he'd hit his daughter, but he couldn't forgive the bastard for hurting Toni. Even now, the jerk talked down to her, questioning her sanity in choosing to marry a rodeo bum and to have a baby so early in her marriage. He'd had enough of the man's destructive barbs.

"Mr. Swenson, I'd suggest you shut your mouth." Brand tossed the ice bag on the table and stepped between his father-in-law and Toni. The room grew silent. "I don't like bullies and from what I've seen, that's what you are. If you have a problem with me or my career, then you talk to me, but get off Toni's case."

Like most bullies, Paul Swenson backed down when confronted. Lips thinned, he sat down in a chair. Toni's mother stood behind him, squeezing his shoulders. Brand had to wonder why she put up with the man. He sighed and ran a hand over his face. This was not the way to get to know his in-laws. The man might be a jackass, but he *was* Toni's father.

"If you have questions, ask me," he repeated. "Toni's not up to an inquisition right now. If anything, you should be concerned about her and the baby, not about whether or not we knew each other's favorite color before we married."

Brand took in Toni's pale face, covered in a light sheen of sweat. Her lips were pinched and pale, and she looked as if she was going to be sick again. "You all right, darlin'?"

Slapping a hand over her mouth, Toni shook her head and bolted from the kitchen. Brand followed. She bent over the toilet and heaved. Brand knelt down to hold her hair out of the way. He'd had a lot of experience with drunk, heaving cowboys. A heaving woman wasn't that different, was it? Only, with his buddies he didn't feel this helpless.

When Toni finished rinsing her mouth, Brand dampened the hand towel and gently wiped her face. The colorful bruise stood out on her ashen skin. Guilt kicked him hard. His bulls. His fault. He'd forced himself on her as a husband and ramrodded his ideas for the ranch down her throat. Was he any less of a bully than her father? He brushed his lips over her cheek. "I'm sorry."

She touched his swollen chin. "Me, too."

The tenderness he felt toward the woman he'd married felt strange, like a pair of unbroken-in boots. It would take some getting used to.

"Sweet tea and toast, coming up. It's what my wife always had to settle her stomach," Rusty called out.

Her father turned when they entered the kitchen. "Did the appraiser come out? He told me he'd get a value and contact the real-estate agent."

Toni's parents wanted her to sell out. A hard knot formed in Brand's stomach. "Toni and I aren't selling."

Toni's father glared in Brand's direction. "We want you to move home with us, Toni."

Brand stiffened and clenched his fists. He wasn't letting this abusive bastard near Toni or their baby. "She *is* home."

"How long have you known this man?" Swenson glared in Brand's direction.

"We met last month in Vegas," Toni admitted quietly.

"And which college did you attend, Lander?"

Brand flexed his fingers under the table and suppressed the urge to knock out the man's teeth. "I didn't."

"Did you even finish high school before you took off chasing rainbows?"

Brand gritted his teeth.

"Dad—"

Her father turned an angry red. "Do you think this no-good cowboy married you for love? Use your head, girl. He married you for your land and that degree of yours. You're his meal ticket. Cowboys know how to spend money. They don't know how to make it."

Brand put his fist down on the table hard enough to rattle the dishes. Toni nearly jumped out of her chair. "I married your daughter for several reasons. Money was not one of them."

"I appreciate your concern, Dad, but I don't need it."

"You rushed into a marriage with a man you barely know," her father said irritably. "Admit it, you made a mistake. Come home and I'll fix it."

Toni shot to her feet. She weaved a little and Brand stood to support her. "I'll never do that and you know it. I'm making a home for my baby here. I want my child to be safe, and I don't think he would be with you."

Swenson looked livid. He pulled out his checkbook. "What will it take to get rid of you, cowboy?"

Brand held on to his temper by a fraying thread. Beneath his hands, he felt Toni tremble. "Mister, you don't have what it takes." He steered Toni toward the door. "Let's go for a walk, darlin'. I think you need some fresh air. I know I do."

Ten

When they reached the pasture fence, Brand caught Toni's arm and turned her toward him. "Why in the hell didn't you tell me about your father?"

Toni gazed toward the cattle off in the distance and fingered the small horseshoe-shaped scar on her chin. He'd kissed it dozens of times. Brand's gut tightened in anger when he remembered that her father had been wearing a ring with a small horseshoe made out of diamonds on it. The bastard.

"What was I supposed to say? 'By the way, my dad likes to hit women'?" Toni hooked her boot over the peeling white fence.

"Tell me the rest of it."

She looked hesitant, then resigned. "My dad is a control freak. Whenever things didn't go exactly as he wanted, he took his anger out on us. I tried to take the brunt of it. Better me than Mom."

"He should have been locked up. You should have told someone."

Toni turned to face him and the defeat in her eyes hit Brand like a blow to the gut. "I tried to get help. I talked to the school counselors a couple of times and they made noises about calling in Social Services. But the wheels turn slow. Before they could do anything, Dad would change jobs. That meant new states, new schools, losing the few friends I'd made. It got so that he'd move us whenever he thought I was getting too close to anyone. He didn't want to risk me talking."

Brand swore. No wonder Toni was made of steel.

"The moving and physical abuse were his way of keeping Mom and I in line. As long as we had no one else, he was our only security, our only constant. The only place I felt safe was here on the Rocking A." She turned and gripped his arm. Her face was pale and drawn, and he wanted to pull her into his arms and hold her tight. "Brand, he is my father and even though he is a jerk I love him. For a long time I was convinced if I'd been a better daughter, none of it would have happened."

"Toni, he's sick."

"I know that now. The last time he hurt me I ended up in the hospital. It took a persistent counselor who met me on the sly to convince me that it wasn't my fault. She's the one who told me that I couldn't help my mother if she didn't want to be helped. She's the one who convinced me to leave.

"If what my mom says about Dad getting help is the truth, then it's a start. He's never been willing to admit he had a problem before."

"He hurt you." Frustration and anger burned Brand's chest.

"Yes, he did. But what hurt more was that no matter how much my grandfather and I begged, my mother wouldn't leave. She said she couldn't take my grandfather trying to run her life the way he had when she was younger.'' Toni's laugh held no humor. ''What Mom didn't realize was that my father was ten times worse. Granddad may have been bossy and he did like to keep us close to home, but he did it to protect us, not to control us. And he never, ever laid a hand on me in anger.''

A lump in Brand's throat threatened to choke him. Toni needed the ranch. She'd told him that before, but he hadn't understood the level of her commitment. Now he did. And did he have it in his heart to force himself on her at the cost of her happiness?

Some of her father's condemning words replayed in Brand's head. What did he have to offer a woman with a graduate degree? Money and a willingness to work hard seemed to be his only assets. He'd never gone to college, never held a steady job other than bull riding. Toni deserved better.

Her parents' car was gone. Toni heaved a sigh of relief and let herself into the house.

Brand followed, carrying an armload of wood. ''Let's build a fire and decorate the tree. Rusty said he'd put it in the stand.''

The tree filled the corner of the den, its scent permeating the air. Beside it sat the familiar box holding her grandmother's Christmas ornaments. Toni knelt beside the box and lifted the lid. A nostalgic smile tilted her mouth. Most of the ornaments were homemade, some she'd made herself. There were crocheted snowflakes, painted pinecones, and tiny knitted stockings. Each was a symbol of her heritage here on the Rocking A. The ornaments were a legacy she'd pass on to her child.

Brand reached into the box and lifted a jar lid bordered in red ribbon. On the flat side, a picture of Santa had been glued. The inside of the lid framed a picture of Toni.

Brand stared at the photo. ''How old were you here?''

Toni wrinkled her nose at the toothless mug shot. ''Seven. That was the year I begged Santa for front teeth.

Grandma made one of those each year until she died. There should be sixteen of them.''

''You spent a lot of time here.'' Brand stood to untangle the lights.

''Summers and every long holiday. Dad worked in hotel management and he could never leave the hotels on holidays. He didn't want a child running through the halls disturbing the guests. I later realized my grandparents had me here because Dad was under a lot of pressure during those times and it was better if I wasn't around. I didn't mind. I loved it here, and I don't ever want to leave again.'' Toni sat back on her heels cradling an angel made from the remnants of her great-great-grandmother's wedding dress. ''What did your family do for Christmas?''

Brand dug into the box, his face turned away from her, but the angle of his jaw was tight. ''Not much after Mom left. It was just another day. Stock had to be tended. Stalls needed cleaning. Dad did the best he could, but money was tight.''

He carried a strand of lights to the tree without glancing her way. Toni's heart ached for the little boy who'd had no Christmas. ''What about Santa?''

''He quit coming after Mom left.''

Tears stung her eyes, but the stiffness in his shoulders told her Brand wouldn't accept pity. There was one special gift she could give her husband. Christmas.

Early Christmas morning, Brand sneaked out of bed and down the stairs. Even at 6:00 a.m., the air smelled of roasting turkey. The kitchen counters were covered in pies, cakes and sugar cookies. It had been a long time, but he remembered the holidays before his mother left. Like Toni, his mother had spent days preparing and had risen before dawn to put the bird in the oven.

His gut twisted. He wanted to believe in forever, even felt a flicker of hope that maybe Toni would be different from the other women in his life. But he was afraid to trust the feeling. Afraid to set himself up for another disappointment.

He swiped a cookie while the milk heated. Juggling a thermos of hot chocolate and one large present, he returned upstairs, stopping in the bedroom doorway.

Toni stood in front of the window, stretching. Sunlight shone directly through the sheer nightgown she wore, outlining her curves in a way that had his body responding with enthusiasm. He set the present in the center of the bed and poured her a mug of hot chocolate. "Merry Christmas."

"To you, too. Thanks." Toni took the mug and sipped it.

He pulled his thoughts from his throbbing groin and nodded toward the box. "You might want to open that one right away."

As eager as a child, Toni scampered onto the bed and ripped the wrapping paper. She hesitated when she read the cardboard box then her lips turned up. "You bought me a case of crackers?"

"The lady at the grocery store suggested it. Said crackers were the only thing that settled her stomach when she was expecting."

Toni laughed, opened a box, and started nibbling. "I guess I don't have to feel bad about giving you this then." She reached under the bed, pulled out a flat package, and tossed it to him.

Brand tore the wrapping paper and read the cover of the book. Was she making fun of his cowardice? "It's about snakes."

"The book has every species of snake, whether or not it's poisonous, and where its territory is located. I thought it might help you get past your fear if you knew which ones could hurt you and which wouldn't."

Brand grimaced at the reminder of his disgrace, but at least she wasn't laughing at him. "Uh...thanks."

"You're welcome. The rest of your gifts are downstairs."

Snatching up her robe, she skipped downstairs. She gave him chambray work shirts, socks and a rifle. "In case the book doesn't help," she said with a grin. "Either Rusty or I can give you marksmanship lessons."

Brand glanced at the presents still under the tree. The crew, except for Rusty, had left to spend Christmas with their families. "Who're those for?"

She took a deep breath and blew it out, eyeing him warily. "Your family. I invited them for Christmas dinner."

Brand kissed her because she was giving him and his family back Christmas. Because she was taking time to try to help him with his snake phobia. Because she'd noticed the holey condition of his socks. Toni was like that. She noticed details. Mostly, he kissed her because he loved her. His love was his secret gift to her. He ruffled her hair. "You have another present. I'll get it."

"Brand, you've already given me the four-wheeler and the cell phone and a year's supply of crackers. What else do I need?"

He held up his finger and retrieved the box from the back porch. He set it in her lap.

Toni lifted the lid. Sleeping inside the box were a fluffy butter-colored kitten and a scraggly mostly black tabby. They wore homemade name tags on the bows tied around their necks. "You named the cats Day and Night? Oh, Brand."

"I like these better than snakes to get rid of the rats in the barn," he explained.

"Me, too." Her smile was like sunshine breaking through the clouds after a week-long rain. It warmed him and made his heart miss a beat. More than that, it made him wish for a hundred more Christmas mornings with Toni, and that was a Christmas wish he was pretty damned certain wasn't going to come true.

* * *

Toni opened the front door to the four Lander men. With a sense of déjà vu she noted their somber expressions. Cort came forward with a sprig of mistletoe in his hand. He held it over her head and gave her a peck on the cheek. "Merry Christmas, sis."

The youngest son had the holiday spirit the others sorely lacked. Toni invited them in and introduced them to Rusty.

"Holy smoke. She's invited Santa," Toni heard Patrick grumble. "Where's Brand?"

"Right here," Brand responded. "Bringing in the eggnog. Take your coats off and kick back. Toni won't let us eat until all the presents have been opened."

The men looked pained, but, like children, their eyes lit when they spotted the presents under the tree. It made the effort worth it. Her kittens cavorted amongst the presents, mangling ribbons. When Brand grabbed her hand and pulled her onto the sofa beside him she snuggled into the crook of his arm. It felt right to be here in front of the fire, surrounded by Brand's family—even if Brand's attentiveness could be an act. She hoped it wasn't. The only gift she really wanted was to know that this was the first of many Christmases with Brand.

While they opened presents, Toni discovered that Patrick had a wicked sense of humor, much like Brand's, which slipped out occasionally. Caleb shared Brand's strong sense of responsibility. She especially liked the tales they told.

"Dad was always trying to make our presents, cuz money was tight, ya know," said Caleb. "We tried to do the same thing. I'll never forget the year Patrick got bitten by that rattler he wanted to make into a belt."

"A belt? I thought it was for my lunch box," Brand said.

Caleb and Patrick exchanged chagrined smiles. "We just told you that to scare you. Patrick wanted to make a snakeskin belt for Dad."

"Hell, Brand, we liked to scare ya. We didn't ever intend to kill ya," added Patrick.

While the brothers exchanged insults, Toni stood and walked to the tree. Only one gift remained—the one she'd spent days pulling together. She passed it to Jack Lander. He looked surprised, but peeled off the paper as eagerly as a five-year-old. His large scarred hand swept over the leather binder inside. "What's this?"

"My grandfather had at least a dozen years' worth of rodeo magazines in the attic. I went through them and cut out all the articles and pictures of Brand. I didn't know if you'd kept a scrapbook of his career. One day, I'm hoping you'll show it to your grandkids and tell them what Brand was like growing up."

Jack Lander mashed his lips shut and nodded his head. Toni thought she saw tears in his eyes. After several silent moments, he met her gaze. "I'd like that."

"Kids? Does that mean what I think it means?" asked Cort.

She felt Brand's presence behind her then his arms circled her waist. "It means that we're going to have a baby in the house next Christmas."

Patrick and Caleb exchanged a dark glance. Their lips tightened and their eyes narrowed. Cort, on the other hand, seemed pleased. "Cool. I guess that means you'll get to play Santa again. Just like you did for me all those years."

Toni twisted in Brand's arms and saw the flush on his cheeks. Another piece of the puzzle fell into place and she knew why the youngest Lander still had the Christmas spirit. Brand had kept the tradition alive.

Jack Lander cleared his throat. "Now, can we eat? I'm 'bout starving for some of that cheesecake I saw on the way in."

Toni laughed and turned for the kitchen. "Then I guess we'd better eat."

Brand's father stopped him with a hand on the arm, but

he didn't say another word until the others had left the room. "Your momma would've liked Toni."

Brand couldn't have been more surprised if his father had stripped naked and danced around the tree. "She wouldn't have cared what kind of wife I had."

Sadness filled his father's eyes. "She would've cared. Your momma loved you boys. It was me she couldn't stand. I kept her tied to me when she loved somebody else."

Brand's vocal cords were paralyzed. His father stared at the tree and continued talking. "Your mother and I were just friends. We had too much to drink one night and I got her pregnant. She had nobody else to turn to, so she married me. We had some good years, and I grew to love that woman.

"Once Caleb and Patrick went off to school, your momma got bored stuck at the ranch all day. She took a part-time job in town and she fell for her boss. I knew she was thinking about leaving me." He pulled on his ear which had turned as red as his cheeks. "Your momma couldn't take the pill. I tampered with the condoms and she got pregnant again. She knew her lover wouldn't want her when she was carrying my kid. So she stayed, but she wasn't happy. I convinced her another baby would fix our marriage and we had Cort. But then one day she didn't come home. She'd gone to meet her lover. She left me a note saying she'd send for you and Cort, but she didn't because she and her fella were killed in a car accident down in Mexico."

Remorse etched lines on his face. "Toni seems like a nice girl. Treat her right." He pounded Brand's shoulder and headed toward the kitchen.

Brand couldn't move. His father's words had crumbled his foundations. Everything he'd ever believed about his mother was a lie.

On the day after Christmas, Toni cautiously rolled over in bed, reaching for the crackers on the bedside table even before she opened her eyes. Her head was pounding. On second thoughts, it wasn't coming from inside her head, but from outside the window. She eased herself upright. When the contents of her stomach didn't race for her throat, she shuffled toward the bathroom, munching a cracker along the way. The kittens followed, tripping all over themselves. So far, they hadn't made it out to the barn.

After a shower and toast, she stepped outside to track down the hammering. To her surprise, Brand's brothers were perched on the barn roof. Jack Lander supervised the men scattered around the yard mending the board fence or painting the house.

"Roy, where's Brand and what's going on?"

Roy paused in unloading an armload of paint cans from the bed of Brand's truck. "Your neighbors and in-laws showed up demanding we let 'em help get the place back in shape. Ain't that a kick? Less than a month ago, he couldn't hire nobody. Now that they've seen how much he cares about you—you know, that Prince Charming to the rescue thing when the gate whomped you?—they want to work."

Toni covered the ache that formed in her chest at Roy's words with her hand. Her neighbors and in-laws didn't know it was the baby Brand was really concerned about. If only he cared about her in that way, she would be impossibly happy.

"Brand's down at the bull pen. A couple of boys showed up wanting lessons. Come on. I'll walk with ya." Roy set the cans down and headed for the pens.

Like a flashback, Toni heard the whiskey-rough voice. "Shoulders square. Free hand out front. Concentrate on the basics and you'll do fine."

"I'd sure like to see you ride him, Brand," a boy of perhaps eighteen said with an eagerness that made Toni's stomach clench in apprehension. Would Brand ride? In

Vegas, she hadn't cared about the risks he took, but now...for the baby's sake, *for her sake,* she hoped he wouldn't ride.

"I rode him in Cheyenne for ninety-two points. Be glad to show you the video sometime, but I'm not getting back on him. I've got a baby on the way, Chris, and I plan to live to see the kid through college." Brand slapped the boy's protective leather vest. "Run like hell when you hit the ground."

"Yeah, yeah, I know." Chris turned toward the chute where Aaron and Deke waited with a bull.

As if sensing her presence, Brand turned. His eyes swept her, then he nodded. "Morning, ma'am. You're looking good today." He stepped closer and brushed his thumb over her lips. The heat in his eyes told her he was wishing it were his mouth. So was she. "As a matter of fact, Mrs. Lander, you look *damn* good."

Toni felt a blush warm her and take some of the chill off her heart. "You're looking mighty fine yourself."

"We're ready, Brand," called Deke.

"Gotta go." He pressed his lips against her forehead, then turned toward the chute.

Roy climbed down off the fence and stood beside her while Brand coached the kid from beside the chute. "He's really good with the boys. O'course none of them have made the count, but they're just high-school kids."

The chute opened. Dirt, bull and cowboy flew through the air. Aaron and Deke played rodeo clown, heading the bull off and turning it into the holding pen. Once the bull was penned, Brand climbed over the fence. He coached the kid on his good moves, then pointed out his mistakes. He finished with another positive comment. From the expression on the boy's face, Toni could tell he hung on Brand's every word and left the ring encouraged, not discouraged. She had to admit Brand was a good teacher.

"This bull-riding school of Brand's could be a real moneymaker." Roy narrowed his eyes on her; his usual flirtatious manner was lacking. "That is, if he don't have to give it up."

"I'm not making him give it up."

"Hope not. He's already quit riding for you. I'd hate to see him lose this, too. A woman can only take so much from a man before he ain't the man she wanted to begin with."

Roy ambled away and Toni stared after him. She didn't want to change Brand. She admired his courage, his honesty and his strong sense of responsibility—qualities she hadn't wanted when she'd gone hunting for a cowboy in Vegas. Brand Lander was definitely not the man she'd wanted to begin with, but for whatever reason, he was the man fate had chosen to father her child and steal her heart. She'd never regret their time together.

Brand waved goodbye to the boys, then climbed out of the empty ring. He strode in her direction. Anticipation fizzed through her bloodstream at the look of intent on his face. He caught her hand, dragged her into the tractor shed and slanted his lips across hers in a kiss so thorough it left her breathless and weak in the knees. She clung to his broad shoulders to stay on her feet.

He lifted his head. "Whaddaya say we take a lunch break?"

Heat pooled in Toni's belly at the sensual promise in Brand's eyes. She dampened her lips. "It might be a little tricky slipping away with a dozen or so men in the yard."

His grin widened. "But not impossible."

Someone in the yard yelled. Metal clanged. Brand was out of the shed in an instant. Toni followed one step behind. She made it to the clearing just in time to see the black bull lunge out of the chute with Wade clinging to his pitching back.

"Sonofabitch." Brand launched himself over the fence. Aaron and Deke did the same. A scream lodged itself in Toni's throat. Neither Brand, Aaron nor Deke wore their protective vests. Within seconds, Wade was airborne. He hit the ground hard and the bull turned on him. Brand threw his hat and waved his arms, distracting the bull from Wade. When it turned toward him, he ran toward the rails with the bull on his heels. Toni's muscles locked with fear. When it looked certain the black beast would hook Brand, Deke ran between them. The bull veered after him. Deke made it into the holding pen just yards ahead of the beast and launched himself up the metal fence. Aaron slammed the gate closed and latched it shut.

Toni's heart hammered and her stomach pitched. It had happened so fast. Brand had nearly been gored and then—

Wade released his hold on the rails and stepped back down into the dirt. Toni'd never seen Brand look so angry. In seconds he'd crossed the ring, grabbed Wade by the shirt, and shoved him against the metal rails. "What in the hell were you doing? Are you outta your mind?"

Toni was afraid, afraid of the anger she saw in her husband's face, afraid of what he would do if she didn't divert his rage from the young cowboy. She clambered over the fence and tried to shove herself between Brand and Wade.

"Brand, stop." She grabbed his forearm and pulled with all her might, but she wasn't able to move him.

Brand ignored her. He glared at Wade. "You coulda gotten yourself killed."

"Brand, please." She tried again.

"If you're going to pull asinine stunts like that, then you pack your bags and get the hell off my ranch. I'm not in the suicide business."

"He was trying to impress you," she shouted. Dark brown eyes shifted her way then back toward the cowering Wade.

"You put Aaron, Deke and I—three men—at risk for a joyride. Do you think that's gonna impress anybody?"

Wade cowered.

Brand's face was flushed, but pale around the lips. His body trembled with fury. He looked livid, but still he didn't raise a hand to Wade. Or her. Tension eased from

Toni's shoulders. She relaxed her hold on his arm, knowing she'd probably caused bruises. Even though the young cowboy could have gotten any of them injured or worse, Brand seemed more interested in scaring the daylights out of him than in hurting him.

"I...I'm sorry," Wade stammered.

"Sorry don't mean squat if you can't back it up with action. I can't work with a man I can't trust, Wade."

"Yessir." Wade bowed his head.

"You know the rules. No bullfighters, no rides."

"Yessir. I was stupid."

Brand sighed and rubbed his temple. "You're not stupid, kid. You made one bad choice. Don't let it happen again."

Toni watched the group disperse with no blood shed. Her father had belted her and her mother for far less serious offenses. Were the counselors right? Were there men out there who knew how to control their anger? Was Brand one of them?

Once the ring cleared out, Brand glanced her way. He narrowed his lips. "You thought I was going to hit him."

She considered denying it, but nodded instead.

He swore. "I'm not your father, Toni."

"I'm beginning to see that."

"Is that what you did? Put yourself between your mother and father when they fought?"

"Somebody had to protect her."

He pulled her into his arms and buried his face in her hair. "It should have been the law, not an innocent kid."

Eleven

Toni set down the phone and paced the office. Megan Jeffries from Coyote Western Wear in Houston had just called. Brand's sponsors. Brand's former lover. She wanted him there for an entire week for a product shoot.

Toni's hands were shaking. She felt weak and it had nothing to do with her pregnancy. She'd let herself fall in love with her one-night cowboy, and she no longer wanted him to leave. Instead of counting the days until he lost interest and left her, she now feared he'd do exactly that. She wanted Brand for keeps.

Brand, on the other hand, saw her as a temporary sexual partner, the incubator for his child and the co-owner of the ranch. A necessary evil. He chivvied endlessly. "Don't lift that. It's too heavy. You might hurt the baby. Don't climb that. You'll fall and hurt the baby. Don't forget to drink your milk. It's good for the baby."

He'd taken to reading and quoting books on pregnancy and childbirth. If he loved her and not just the child she carried, Toni would have been thrilled by his interest. She was jealous of her own baby. Add another sin to her growing list.

She sank into the leather chair and put her head in her hands. Her own experiences had taught her that keeping someone under lock and key wasn't the way to hold on to them. She had to let Brand go to Houston. She had to trust him not to break her heart.

Boots rapped out a staccato rhythm on the hardwood floor of the hall. Brand entered the office with Craig Stevens on his tail.

"The doc is back to make you another offer." Brand's voice was flat, his eyes expressionless.

"He's right, Toni. I am here to make you another offer, but first, congratulations on the baby."

"Thanks." Toni put a hand over her abdomen and smiled. Patting the baby was becoming as much a habit as eating crackers. As they always did, Brand's eyes followed the gesture.

Dr. Stevens sat down. "First, I want to assure you both that what I need Toni to do won't be hazardous. I need help in the surgery. I've ordered new laser equipment and don't know how to use it. I'd appreciate some help setting it up and some tutoring. How do you feel about teaching an old dog new tricks?"

Brand saw the excited sparkle in Toni's blue eyes, the pink flush on her cheek. It faded to disappointment and resignation.

"I appreciate the offer, but I want to start a breeding program and I won't be able to spare the time," Toni said.

Dr. Stevens frowned at Brand. "You can't spare her for say…fifteen hours a week?"

Toni answered before Brand could open his mouth. "No, the beef operation is mine. Brand is working with his bulls."

She wanted the job and he wanted her to stay. Hell, he

could handle a little extra work and hire a few extra hands if it would make her happy. "I'll cover for you."

He'd bet that Toni's smile couldn't get any wider. She launched herself at him. He caught her in his arms and squeezed her tight, savoring her joy and hating that he had to let her out of his sight.

A beeping noise pierced the silence. The vet fumbled for the pager hooked to his belt. "Do I take that as a yes, Toni?"

"You bet."

"Stop by the office Monday morning, and we'll get started."

The doctor's bootsteps faded down the hall. As quickly as it had erupted, Toni's smile vanished. She crossed the room and stared out the window. "You had a call while you were out."

Puzzled by her sudden mood swing, Brand propped his hip on the desk and studied her stiff spine. "Yeah?"

"Megan Jeffries wants you to call her at home. She said she'd need you to stay in Houston all of next week."

"Next week? I thought that was…" Time flew when he was with Toni. "I'll call later. Right now I have something more important to tend to."

He caught her hand as she tried to leave the room, pulled her between his thighs. Something about Megan's call had upset her. He wanted to hash it out. Toni squirmed in his hold. She scowled and tugged on her hand, but Brand held tight. He turned her until her back rested against his chest, and then he leaned forward to inhale the sweet scent of her hair, of her.

"You want to tell me what has you all knotted up?" Beginning at her stiff shoulders, he massaged his way down her spine. Whenever Toni worried she knotted up.

"Nothing."

"Uh-huh. Do you have a problem with me going to Houston?"

"Of course not." She was lying through her pretty

white teeth. Toni turned and tried to step away. He snagged a couple of her belt loops with his fingers, trapping her between his legs, and massaged the curve of her waist with his thumbs.

She pretended not to notice, but the flush on her cheeks and the catch in her breath were hard to miss. She reached past him to search through the papers on the desk to his left. If he didn't know better, he'd think she was jealous. But he knew better, didn't he?

"Toni, you don't have to worry about Megan."

She redirected her search to the papers on his right.

"It's been over for a long time." She continued to shuffle through the stack as if she'd lost something vital. "Since before the season started last—"

She held up her hand as if she didn't want to hear more. "I can't find my college-loan payment book. I thought I put it in the desk drawer."

Brand traced a path along the inside of her waistband and up her rib cage. Touching Toni had its usual effect. He shifted her against his arousal. After a quick gasp of surprise, she leaned into him, giving him one of her mind-blowing kisses. When her nipples pebbled and poked against her shirt he just had to touch 'em.

"I paid off your loan." He whispered the words against her temple.

She jerked her head up so fast she clipped his chin. He nearly bit his tongue. "Why?"

Brand shrugged and cupped her shoulders. "I wanted to. Didn't make much sense for you to pay interest on the loan when I had the money sitting in the bank to pay it off."

For a moment, he thought she'd argue. Her brow puckered. "Thank you. I'll put it toward your half of the ranch."

He pulled her shirttail free to stroke the soft skin beneath. He wanted to tell her that she was the only woman in his life, and she wouldn't even look at him. "Come with me to Houston."

Her muscles quivered beneath his fingertips. "I—I'm supposed to start work on Monday."

Brand smothered his disappointment. "Yeah, I forgot. No big deal. I'll only be gone a week."

But it was a big deal. He didn't want to leave her. He considered trying to change her mind. This His and Hers business had to stop. They were a team—at least for now.

Toni nibbled his neck and lowered his zipper. Brand sucked a sharp breath and forgot about arguing when she freed him from the restricting denim and took him into her mouth. For precious moments, Brand let her have her way, although the pleasure nearly took his head off. He scooted off the desk and fumbled with the snap and zipper of her jeans. Once he'd peeled the snug denim away, he laid her on her back across the desk and buried himself within her slick heat.

Toni wriggled and wrapped her legs around his waist. He loved it when she played aggressively. As if reading his thoughts, she grabbed his shirt collar in her fists and pulled him down for a kiss. Damn, the woman knew how to kiss. Her lips teased his. Her teeth nipped, then her sweet little tongue swept the inside of his bottom lip.

Some corner of his mind told him there was a hint of desperation in her loving, but when she popped open the snaps of his shirt and scraped her short nails over his chest he lost his train of thought. Brand drew back to return the favor. He flicked open the front fastening of her bra and pulled a pink-tipped breast into his mouth. She was even more sensitive there now and when he nipped her she made the sexiest noise he'd ever heard. He made her do it again.

Shock waves radiated through his body. He clutched her hips. "Slow down. I'm on the edge here."

She writhed beneath him. "Mmm, me too."

Brand leaned over to tease her plump breasts. He suckled and bit in the way he knew drove her wild. With his thumb, he teased the heart of her until she exploded, her body arching off the desk, squeezing him. Brand gave in and rode the crest with her.

While he struggled to catch his breath, he tugged her into sitting position and refastened her bra and shirt. His fingers wandered and it took a little longer than it should have.

"We've got to stop meeting like this." He jerked his head to indicate the office door they'd left wide open. The woman made him forget good ol' common sense sometimes. The men were due in for lunch soon, and he'd rather not have the guys see Toni like this. They were already half in love with her. If they saw her looking this sexy he'd definitely need Toni's marksmanship lessons to keep 'em in line.

Biting her lips on a wicked smile, she slapped the door closed. "You started it."

Brand couldn't help but grin right back at her. He stepped back so she could scoot off the desk. "Who me? I didn't do anything."

She shimmied into her jeans, glancing over her shoulder at him. "Will you not do anything again sometime soon?"

He had to clamp down on his baser instincts. Otherwise, he'd be stripping her right back out of those britches. A mess of work waited for him outside, but he sat down in the chair behind the desk and pulled her into his lap. She laid her head on his shoulder and rested her hand over his heart. It was times like this that made him forget how they'd started and how they'd likely end up. Apart.

"This'll probably be my last trip to Houston." He had enough money to do what he wanted. His contract with Coyote Western Wear was almost up, and he wouldn't renew it. It was time to turn the endorsements over to one of the younger riders who wouldn't mind being away from home—away from family.

"That's good—um, are you sure?"

"Yeah." He stroked a path from her silky lips to her cotton-covered belly. "We'll be busy around here."

Toni ducked her head. "Yeah." She fiddled with the snap on his shirt. "Thanks for agreeing to help with the breeding program."

Whatever it takes to keep you here. He almost said the words aloud.

Toni sat beside Brand as he drove them toward town. She brushed the crumbs off her shirt. She'd been eating crackers to settle her antsy stomach ever since the call from Kyle Williams, her lawyer. Something wasn't right, but Kyle refused to discuss it over the phone. He'd insisted they make an appointment before Brand went out of town. The urgency doubled her nervousness.

The receptionist ushered them straight into Kyle's office. Toni introduced the men and took a seat even though sitting was the last thing she wanted to do. The tight look on Kyle's face didn't bode well. "What's the problem?"

Kyle pushed his glasses up on his nose and steepled his fingers. "As we discussed, you had to have a male heir to gain control of your grandfather's ranch." Toni nodded cautiously.

"Toni, you should have talked to me before taking such drastic measures."

"You were gone a month. I talked to Tom. Your partner drew up our prenuptial agreement."

Kyle shuffled the papers in his hands. "I advised your grandfather against the clause, but he insisted. I'm afraid my partner didn't fully understand the terms when he drew up your prenuptial agreement."

The crackers in Toni's stomach turned to lead. Scooting toward the edge of the chair, she gripped the edge of his desk. "What are you saying?"

Kyle glanced at Brand then fixed his somber gaze on Toni. "Even though you're expecting, the wedding came before the birth of a child. It takes precedence." He paused. Toni's heart did the same. "The deed to the ranch must go into your husband's name." He shook his head. "I'm sorry you didn't get the copy of the will I mailed to your apartment. At least then you might have had a chance to read it before taking such drastic measures."

She could only stare at Kyle in disbelief. This sick feeling in her stomach intensified.

"Toni, I liked and respected your grandfather, but we both know how he felt about a woman running a ranch, or he would have left the place to your mother. Will wanted you to find a husband and settle down. He thought this would hurry you and Josh to the altar."

She might pass out. "What you're saying is that by marrying Brand I didn't gain control of the ranch. *I gave it away?*"

"More or less, yes."

Through the buzzing in her ears she heard Brand ask, "You're saying the ranch is mine?"

"Correct."

A cold sweat dampened her forehead. Spots clouded her vision. She'd sold herself for a piece of land and come up with nothing. She straightened. No, that wasn't right. She'd have her baby. They just wouldn't have a home.

Brand leaned forward in his chair, apparently eager to take it all from her. He wouldn't have to keep her in order to own the land. He'd probably kick her off the ranch and try to take their child away from her, too.

"What you're saying is that I can do anything I want with the property? Sell it, develop it? List the deed anyway I see fit?"

"That is correct." Kyle's tone grew frostier.

This was the payback for all the sins she'd committed. God or Fate or whoever held the cards was playing a cruel trick. Just when she thought she had it all, it was being wrenched from her fingers. She was going to be sick.

Brand leaned back, crossed his ankles, and smiled. That cunning smile made Toni's heart turn over. She'd played the game and lost. She stumbled to her feet and headed for the door. Brand jumped up, but she waved him off. She needed to be alone. "Ladies' room."

Brand stared at the closed door, concern over Toni's pallor making him want to follow. "She has morning sickness at the damnedest times."

"I'll have my secretary check on her."

Still worried, Brand sat back down while the attorney directed his secretary to keep an eye on Toni.

"Brand, I need to know what you intend to do with the ranch."

"Put Toni's name on the deed."

The attorney narrowed his eyes. "If you mean her name alone, then I'd have to point out that wouldn't be a sound move financially. You'd pay inheritance taxes, and then she would be taxed again on the same property."

"Counselor, if you bothered to read the prenup your partner drew up, you'd know Toni and I want a fifty-fifty split. You might not think it was a legally binding agreement, but I signed it and I intend to respect it."

Brand glanced at the door and stood. Toni hadn't come back. "While you're fixing that, we'll need to set up a trust fund for this baby and change my will to name Toni and the child as beneficiaries."

For the first time since their arrival, Brand saw respect in the man's gaze. Kyle stood and offered Brand his hand. "I'll have the papers ready for your signature when you return from your trip. It'll be a pleasure doing business with you, Mr. Lander."

The secretary peeked in. "Mrs. Lander has left. She asked me to call a cab to take you to the airport."

Brand wandered around the arena, surprised that the itch to compete hadn't hit him the minute he'd walked through the gate. His buddies razzed him about tying the knot, and he took it. He'd missed these people, but tonight all he could think about was that Toni hadn't answered the phone when he'd called from the airport.

"Hello, gorgeous."

Brand turned. Megan was as beautiful as ever, but he didn't feel the need to press his lips to hers or grind his chest against her ample bosom. "Hey, Meg."

She twined her fingers around his neck, but he turned his head. Her kiss landed on his cheek. "I can't believe you really did it. I thought it was a joke when you told me you got married. You always swore no woman would ever tie you down."

He had, and he'd meant it. "That was before I met Toni."

"Well, wife or no wife, you're mine for the next week. Your retirement is making the marketing department crazy. We've been scrambling for ways to make the most of it before people forget your name. Let's get you suited up before the check presentation."

She followed him into the dressing room just like she always had. Brand had never minded undressing in front of Megan before. "Meg, if you'll tell me what I'm supposed to wear, you can go check on the rest of the setup."

She dragged a finger down his shirt placket. "Need help?"

"Nope."

"Toni's a lucky woman."

"I hope she thinks so. Is there a phone I can use?"

This was crazy. He loved his wife and he hadn't even told her. Maybe if she knew she'd be willing to give him a chance. He shook his head. He'd never told a woman he loved her before and he wanted to see Toni's face when he said the words.

"Hey, Meg, any chance we can wrap this thing up early?"

* * *

Toni rolled the spool of barbed wire toward the back of the four-wheeler.

"I'll do that." Roy grabbed the wire and headed off.

Dusting off her hands, she turned toward the tractor shed determined to start on the seeding. But Aaron was there before she could fire up the motor. "Which pasture you want done?"

"The west one." He started the tractor and drove off.

Parking her hands on her hips, Toni pursed her lips and frowned after him. What was going on? Deke had intercepted when she'd said she was going to ride out to check the herd, claiming he needed something he'd left at the well yesterday. Wade had developed a sudden urge to muck stalls—as soon as he saw the pitchfork in her hands. The men wouldn't let her lift a finger. Any job she'd attempted yesterday and today had been taken over by someone else.

Rusty glanced up from the bench where he was mending a bridle. "They mean well."

Toni figured her frustration must be plainly written on her face. "What's going on?"

He hesitated then set the bridle down. "Brand asked the crew to keep an eye on you while he was gone." Toni's anger stirred. She clenched her fists and pinched her lips. "Ain't no reason to get riled, Toni-girl. Brand don't understand that he's making you feel penned, but he'll learn—if you're willing to teach him."

"So what *am* I allowed to do? Can I leave the yard? Or do I have to sneak around like I did with Granddad?"

"The boy's lookin' out for you the best way he knows how."

"I can look after myself." Toni spun on her heel and marched toward the house. All her old frustrations rose to the surface. She felt trapped, but sitting and stewing wasn't her way. When her grandfather wouldn't give her anything to do, she'd found jobs for herself. If Brand was determined to confine her to the house, she'd work in the house.

It wasn't as if she didn't have plenty to do to get ready for the baby and no nosy cowboys would interfere.

The house was a run-down dump, but a dump she loved with all her heart. She had a week to turn it into the kind of home a man liked to return to. Then maybe Brand wouldn't leave her.

Toni studied the freshly painted sky-blue walls of the nursery, then the paint cans stacked on the floor. She rolled her tired shoulder muscles and flipped through the magazine to the picture she'd earmarked. She'd never painted clouds or a rainbow before, but she'd go nuts if she had to sit around the house and think of Brand with Megan. Working in the vet's office each morning helped, but the afternoons were long and lonely. Even though Brand called every night, she felt restless without him here. He hadn't mentioned the will and she hadn't asked, fearing he'd tell her to be gone before he got home. If only he'd told her he loved her....

Determined to finish the room before Brand got home at the end of the week she pried the lid off the paint can. In the last three days, she'd painted the den, kitchen and master bedroom. The house was shaping up.

The kittens scampered across the room, skidded on the drop cloth, then darted through her legs and scampered up the step stool. She shooed them back down. "Hey, you two, scoot."

Toni poured the paint into the tray and dipped in the rag. According to the magazine, all she had to do was to blot the rag against the tops of the walls. The result should look like puffy white clouds. Climbing up to the third rung, she daubed the paint into a cloudlike shape, then stepped back down to judge her work. Pretty good. Moving the step stool along the wall, she repeated the process. Up. Down. Up. Two clouds done, probably another dozen to go before she made it around the room.

She daubed another cloud and descended. A terrible screech rent the air, and Toni jerked her foot off the tail she'd inadvertently trodden on. The kitten dodged the same way she did. Toni lost her balance, dropped the rag, and windmilled to no avail. The floor rushed at her and the impact of hardwood floor against her hip knocked the breath from her.

Her first thought was of the baby, but surely nothing could happen. She hadn't fallen far. A blob of paint dripped from her hair onto her nose and cheek. Good grief, if Brand could see her now. She needed a shower.

Shoving herself to her feet, she looked for the kittens, but they'd scampered off. A faint trail of white paw prints marked their path. She took the time to mop them up before peeling off her paint-soiled clothes and heading for the bathroom.

The paint blended with the warm water in a milky-colored mix. She lathered her hair and continued to rinse until the water ran clear. The pink streak swirling the drain was unexpected. Confused, she looked down. A thin trail of red ran down her leg. *The baby.* Panic hit her like a truck. Throwing back the shower curtain, she snatched a towel and hastily dried off.

The baby. Something was wrong with her baby. She had to get to a doctor. She had to find Brand.

Pale and tense, she knelt by the phone because her legs were too shaky to support her. First, she called the obstetrician to tell her that she was coming to the hospital. Next, she tried Brand's hotel room. She waited for the beep and left her message.

"Brand, I'm bleeding. I think it's—" Her voice cracked. Toni tried again. "I fell and I think I hurt the baby."

Toni replaced the receiver and pulled her clothes over damp skin. None of the ranch hands were in the yard. She yelled once, but no one answered. Not wanting to waste precious time she scratched out a note and pinned it on the bunkhouse bulletin board. She drove to the hospital as fast as she could. Pulling up to the emergency-room entrance, she threw her keys to one of the men in scrub suits outside and raced through the doors.

Inside, a nurse whisked her behind a curtain. "Your doctor's on her way. Tell me what happened."

Toni focused on her words, not wanting to miss any significant detail. Panic blurred the edges of her sanity. She'd never forgive herself if her stubbornness had caused her to lose the baby. Losing the baby also meant losing Brand.

Brand paced the hospital hallway. He'd never been so scared in all his life. He stopped and looked through the window in the hospital door. Toni lay on the white sheets, so pale she nearly blended into the fabric. The knot in his throat felt as big as his boot, and his eyes burned something fierce. He felt so damned helpless. He shouldn't have left her. He should have stayed home or made her go with him. He shouldn't have asked the guys to keep her from doing the work she loved. Rusty was right. He'd penned her in and she'd rebelled by painting the entire house.

He should have told her he loved her.

"Mr. Lander, your wife was distraught." Brand tried to focus on the doctor who'd stopped beside him. "I gave her something to calm her down. We're trying to be as thorough in our diagnosis as possible. I'm concerned about the bleeding, but I'm not convinced yet that the baby is in danger. We've run some lab tests and—"

"When—" He had to swallow. "When will you know something?" He wanted to get inside to see Toni, but the petite doctor blocked the door as surely as a dam blocked a river.

"The good news is that in the four hours your wife has been here there hasn't been a single contraction. As soon as we can get her to ultrasound, we'll have a better idea of what's going on. Unfortunately, we have to wait for the critical cases to clear out."

He raked a hand through his hair. "You said she was bleeding. Will she be okay? Toni, I mean."

"We'll know soon."

Not soon enough. "Look, get in there and take care of her."

"The baby appears—"

"Dammit, we can have another baby. Take care of my wife." His words stunned him, as did the tears running down his face. Brand clenched his fists and bowed his head. The baby wasn't nearly as important as Toni. Sure, he already loved the little person he hadn't intended to create, but not nearly as much as he loved his wife. There might be other babies, but there would never, *never* be another Toni.

He'd come home early intending to tell her he loved her. Instead, he'd found a panicking crew. They'd shown him Toni's note. Brand shoved off the wall and stared at the doctor. "I need to be with her."

"She'll probably sleep for a few more hours, but you can go in if you promise not to disturb her. You were so upset earlier that I didn't want to let you in until you'd settled down a bit.

"As soon as the ultrasound is available, we'll come for her. For now, be comforted by the fact that the bleeding was sparse and even that has stopped."

The doctor kept on talking, but Brand barely heard her words. His hand trembled when he stroked a path across Toni's cool, colorless cheek to the artery in her neck. He checked her pulse, not trusting the machine that blinked beside her. Tension eased from his shoulders as he felt the steady beat. "Why's that monitor counting over a hundred when her pulse is only sixty beats a minute?"

"That's your baby's heartbeat."

Brand's knees gave out. His butt hit the chair beside the bed. "I-is it supposed to be that fast?"

The doctor patted him on the back. "One hundred twenty is within the normal range."

His child. Toni's child. He slid his hand down her belly to cradle the baby the way he'd seen her do so many times.

Early-morning sunlight stung her eyelids, but Toni didn't want to waken. In her dreams, Brand had held her all night and told her he loved her. He'd stroked her hair, promised her forever and a dozen kids if she wanted them.

Before the dream had been a nightmare of fear. Blurred images of pitying glances, tubes and needles haunted her. Poking and prodding and blood. She hadn't been able to stop crying and she'd asked for Brand until a nurse had injected something into her IV. It could only mean one thing.

Pain pierced her heart. Emptiness threatened to consume her. Tears slid from beneath her lids and dampened her hair. She'd lost her baby and probably Brand, too, because she was a stubborn, pigheaded fool who had to prove her worth.

"Toni?" She turned her head. Brand, looking as awful as she felt, straightened in the chair beside the bed. His face was pale and drawn beneath the black stubble of his morning beard. His hair stuck up in spikes and his clothes were a wreck. For once he wore a solid-black shirt instead of his usual cowboy duds. The somber color seemed appropriate. "How are you, darlin'?"

Her throat blocked up. She couldn't answer. Everything important to her would very likely vanish today. Her hand fluttered over her stomach. She'd never felt so alone. Fresh tears stung her eyes.

Brand took her hand. "You scared the hell out of me."

"I'm sorry. I know that's not enough, but…" How could you apologize for an act of stupidity that cost a man his child? He must hate her.

"Hey, cut that out. I can't stand to see you cry." He brushed at her tears with his thumbs.

"I can't h-help it."

He sat on the bed and pulled her into his arms. How

could he be so tender when she'd done him wrong since day one?

"Do me a favor. No more trips to the hospital until it's time for this little cowpoke to make an appearance."

Toni blinked and drew back. *What?* "The baby…"

"Look, there's its heartbeat, right there." He pointed at the monitor with one hand and pulled her closer with the other. Toni watched the red numbers flash and tried to comprehend what he was saying.

"We're waiting on the ultrasound machine to get a picture of the little critter."

"But I was bleeding."

"The doc says that's not necessarily a bad thing." Brand cupped her cheek. The emotion in his gaze robbed her breath. She had to remind herself that Brand was being attentive because of their child. Dreams didn't really come true, and that wasn't love she saw in his dark eyes. But she wished it were. She put her fist to her mouth to stymie a sob.

"You need some crackers? I can get some from the cafeteria."

Toni blinked away her tears, but her throat burned from the effort of holding back. She hadn't lost her baby. She hadn't lost Brand. *Yet.* When he found out it was her fault that she was here… "I just want to go home."

"As soon as they do the ultrasound I'll check with the doc to see if I can spring you from this place."

The door opened and a nurse walked in. "We're going to take Mommy down the hall. Come on, Dad. If you're good, I'll let you push the chair."

Twenty minutes later Toni gaped at Brand. He looked as stunned as she felt. "Twins?"

The doctor and the ultrasound tech smiled, then the tech pointed out first one beating heart, then another. "It's too early to tell the sex yet, but you can see the hearts are working fine."

The doctor said, "It looks like you just dislodged a little

clot when you fell. Most women hang on to that until closer to labor. Everything else is in the right place for a pair of identical twins.''

Toni looked at the blurry images then at the man beside her. She must have done something right while she'd been racking up all those sins to deserve this. Now all she had to do was find a way to hold on to it.

After a silent ride home Brand carried her inside as if she were fragile and precious. He eased her down onto the bed so gently it made Toni want to weep. She hadn't tried to explain why she'd done what she'd done because she wanted to pretend Brand's love was real for a few more moments.

He stood, shoved his hands into his pants pockets, and turned toward the window. His shoulders rose and fell as he took several deep breaths. Toni braced herself for his well-deserved anger.

''Brand, I—''

''Dammit Toni, I thought I was going to lose you. I…'' He wiped a hand across his face. She saw his Adam's apple bob. ''I hope the nurse took notes. I made so many deals with God I can't remember half of 'em, but I reckon I'll be busy for a while.''

''I know you were worried about the baby….'' Tears choked off her words. She couldn't go on. Coldness seeped into her limbs. More than anything, she wanted to go back to sleep, back to the happy dream. She clutched a pillow to her chest.

''The baby?'' Brand lifted his head with a jerk and approached the bed in quick strides. He reached out and instinctively, Toni's muscles clenched. She forced them to relax because she knew now that Brand would never hurt her—even though she'd pushed him further than any man ought to be pushed.

He brushed the hair off her cheek and tipped her chin up. ''Didn't you hear a word I said last night?'' He sighed and shook his head. Hesitantly, it seemed, he laced his fingers through hers. "Nah, I guess you didn't."

He eased himself down on the edge of the bed and in his eyes made her heart swell with hope. "I was bargaining for you, Toni. For us. Sure, I want these babies, but if…if we lost them, we could try again. If you wanted to."

He touched his lips to hers as soft as a whisper and when he met her gaze his eyes glistened with unshed tears. "I don't want to lose *you*, Toni." He glanced away and cleared his throat. "I had Kyle put your name on the deed. Fifty-fifty. Just like we agreed."

She shouldn't be disappointed when he'd delivered such good news, but for moment she'd thought he was going to say something else. Hoped he was going to say something else. "Thank you. You can't know how much that means to—"

"I love you." He said the words in such a rush and he looked so anxious she thought she'd misunderstood.

"What?"

Brand inhaled deeply and squared his shoulders. The intense concentration on his face resembled the photos of him bull riding that she'd put in his father's scrapbook. "I love you and I don't want to lose you."

Her stomach took a funny turn. "M-me? You love me?"

One corner of his mouth curled upward. "My bossy, opinionated, snake-handling wife? Sure. Who else?"

"I've done you wrong at every turn. How can you love me?"

The teasing smile faded. "There's not another woman who can rile me or excite me or hug me like you do. I'm not willing to give that up."

Joy filled her until she thought she'd burst, but she was still afraid to believe what she'd heard. With an unsteady hand, she stroked his bristly chin. "I love you, too."

A muscle twitched beneath her fingers. Doubt clouded

his eyes. "You're sure? You're not just saying that 'cause I spilled my guts?"

"I went to Vegas looking for a love-'em-and-leave-'em cowboy, but I think I hit the jackpot instead. There's nothing I'd want more than to make a home here with you—and our kids, Brand."

He cupped her face in his hands and met her eyes with a steady gaze. "I want to spend the rest of my life with you, Toni, and God willing, we can have as many kids as you want. As many as your career will allow. You can open up your own practice. We'll build a clinic right on the ranch, and I'll watch the kids while you work."

"And I'll watch them while you work. We'll be one heck of a team."

"Damn straight."

Toni grabbed him by the collar and pulled him forward until their noses touched. She smiled against his lips. "What do you mean *I'm* opinionated?"

Brand's sexy grin was enough to curl her toes. "I notice you're not questioning 'bossy.'"

He gave her one of those slow-building-but-guaranteed-to-fry-her-brain-cells kisses, and Toni knew the sex of their child—children—no longer mattered.

The cowboy who'd followed her home was here to stay.

* * * * *

**Where royalty and romance
go hand in hand...**

The series finishes in

Silhouette

Desire

with these unforgettable love stories:

THE ROYAL TREATMENT
by Maureen Child
October 2002 (SD #1468)

TAMING THE PRINCE
by Elizabeth Bevarly
November 2002 (SD #1474)

ROYALLY PREGNANT
by Barbara McCauley
December 2002 (SD #1480)

Available at your favorite retail outlet.

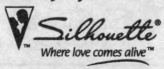

Silhouette ®

Where love comes alive ™

Have you ever wanted to participate in a romance reading group?

Silhouette Special Edition's exciting new book club!

Don't miss

RYAN'S PLACE
by Sherryl Woods

coming in September

Get your friends or relatives together to engage in lively discussions with the suggested reading group questions provided at the end of the novel. Also, visit www.readersring.com for more reading group information!

Available at your favorite retail outlet.

Silhouette®
Where love comes alive™

Delight yourself with four special titles from one of America's top ten romance authors...

USA Today bestselling author

DIANA PALMER

Four passionate and provocative stories that are Diana Palmer at her best!

Sweet Enemy

Love on Trial

Storm Over the Lake

To Love and Cherish

Look for these special titles in September 2002.

Where love comes alive™

October 2002
TAMING THE OUTLAW
#1465 by Cindy Gerard

Don't miss bestselling author
Cindy Gerard's exciting story about
a sexy cowboy's reunion with his
old flame—and the daughter he
didn't know he had!

November 2002
ALL IN THE GAME
#1471 by Barbara Boswell

In the latest tale by beloved
Desire author Barbara Boswell,
a feisty beauty joins her twin as a
reality game show contestant in an
island paradise...and comes face-to-
face with her teenage crush!

December 2002
A COWBOY & A GENTLEMAN
#1477 by Ann Major

Sparks fly when two fiery Texans are
brought together by matchmaking
relatives, in this dynamic story by
the ever-popular Ann Major.

MAN OF THE MONTH

Some men are made for lovin'—and you're sure to love
these three upcoming men of the month!

Available at your favorite retail outlet.

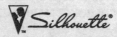

Silhouette *Desire*

presents

DYNASTIES:
THE
CONNELLYS

A brand-new miniseries about the Connellys of Chicago,
a wealthy, powerful American family tied by blood to the
royal family of the island kingdom of Altaria.
They're wealthy, powerful and rocked by
scandal, betrayal…and passion!

Look for a whole year of glamorous and
utterly romantic tales in 2002:

Silhouette®

Where love comes alive™

Beloved author
JOAN ELLIOTT PICKART
introduces the next generation of MacAllisters in

The Baby Bet:
MacAllister's Gifts

with the following heartwarming romances:

On sale July 2002

THE ROYAL MacALLISTER
Silhouette Special Edition #1477
As the MacAllisters prepare for a royal wedding,
Alice "Trip" MacAllister meets her own Prince Charming.

On sale September 2002

PLAIN JANE MacALLISTER
Silhouette Desire #1462
A secret child stirs up trouble—and long-buried
passions—for Emily MacAllister when she is reunited
with her son's father, Dr. Mark Maxwell.

And look for the next exciting installment of
the MacAllister family saga, coming only to
Silhouette Special Edition in December 2002.

*Don't miss these unforgettable romances...
available at your favorite retail outlet.*

Where love comes alive™

COMING NEXT MONTH

#1465 TAMING THE OUTLAW—Cindy Gerard

After six years, sexy Cutter Reno was back in town and wreaking havoc on Peg Lathrop's emotions. Peg still yearned passionately for Cutter—and she wanted to pick up where they had left off. But would he still want her once he learned her precious secret?

**#1466 CINDERELLA'S CONVENIENT HUSBAND—
Katherine Garbera**

Dynasties: The Connellys

Lynn McCoy would do anything to keep the ranch that had been in her family for generations—even marry wealthy Seth Connelly. And when she fell in love with him, Lynn needed to convince her handsome husband they could have their very own happily-ever-after.

#1467 THE SEAL's SURPRISE BABY—Amy J. Fetzer

A trip home turned Jack Singer's life upside down because he learned that beautiful Melanie Patterson, with whom he'd spent one unforgettable night, had secretly borne him a daughter. The honor-bound Navy SEAL proposed a marriage of convenience. But Melanie refused, saying she didn't want him to feel obligated to her. Could Jack persuade her he wanted to be a *real* father...and husband?

#1468 THE ROYAL TREATMENT—Maureen Child

Crown and Glory

Determined to get an interview with the royal family, anchorwoman Jade Erickson went to the palace—and found herself trapped in an elevator in the arms of the handsomest man she'd ever seen. Jeremy Wainwright made her heart beat faster, and he was equally attracted to her, but would the flame of their unexpected passion continue to burn red-hot?

#1469 HEARTS ARE WILD—Laura Wright

Maggie Connor got more than she'd bargained for when she vowed to find the perfect woman for her very attractive male roommate. Nick Kaplan was turning out to be everything *she'd* ever wanted in a man, and she was soon yearning to keep him for herself!

#1470 SECRETS, LIES...AND PASSION—Linda Conrad

An old flame roared back to life when FBI agent Reid Sorrels returned to his hometown to track a suspect. His former fiancée, Jill Bennett, was as lovely as ever, and the electricity between them was undeniable. But they both had secrets....

SDCNM0902